JUST MY LUCK

Olivia feels as if everyone else in her family is perfect. Her mother's just been promoted, her father is finishing his first novel, and her older sister, Drina, has the lead in the school musical. No one has any time for Olivia. And since her best friend Wei Ping moved away, the only people who pay attention to her are old Mr. G, who owns the antique store down the block, and the landlady's goofy-looking nephew, Jeffrey Dingle, who won't leave Olivia alone.

The one thing Olivia wants most is a puppy to love, and she's even found it—a beagle named Cleo. But Cleo costs $200, and if Olivia can't raise the money soon, she's lost her. Then Mrs. Dingle's poodle is stolen. Olivia's determined to collect the $200 reward . . . and Jeffrey's equally determined to help her. Could a new friend be even better than a dog?

JUST MY LUCK

JUST MY LUCK

by Emily Moore

Puffin Books

PUFFIN BOOKS
Published by the Penguin Group
Viking Penguin, a division of Penguin Books USA Inc.,
375 Hudson Street, New York, New York 10014, U.S.A.
Penguin Books Ltd, 27 Wrights Lane, London W8 5TZ, England
Penguin Books Australia Ltd, Ringwood, Victoria, Australia
Penguin Books Canada Ltd, 10 Alcorn Avenue, Toronto, Ontario, Canada M4V 3B2
Penguin Books (N.Z.) Ltd, 182–190 Wairau Road, Auckland 10, New Zealand

Penguin Books Ltd, Registered Offices: Harmondsworth, Middlesex, England

First published in the United States of America by E.P. Dutton, Inc., 1982
Published in Puffin Books, 1991
3 5 7 9 10 8 6 4 2
Copyright © Emily Moore, 1982
All rights reserved

Library of Congress Catalog Card Number: 91-52573
ISBN 0-14-034790-9

Printed in the United States of America
Set in Century Expanded

For my sisters—
Minnie, Carol, and Lucille.
They never stop helping
and supporting.

1

The day started out like all the others—hot, sticky, and borrring! Then the most exciting thing ever in my whole life happened to me. I found out I was getting a puppy.

I've wanted one ever since I can remember. I've read all the dog books in the library. I even sleep with my stuffed beagle, Thomasina, sometimes, hoping I'll wake up one morning to find my parents have surprised me and put a live puppy in place of the toy one.

But I never thought my wish would come true. Not because I'm not old enough to take care of a puppy. I am ten, practically. And it's not because I'm irresponsible. In the last year, I've become the most responsible person I know. Anybody will tell you that.

The reason I thought I'd never get a dog is that both my parents have jobs. Ma is a CPA, which stands for certified public accountant. Since her promotion a few months ago, she's been working twelve hours a day, sometimes more. Daddy is a college English teacher and a part-time writer. That means until I get home from school, no one else is here. Someone has to be around a puppy. It just wouldn't be fair any other way. So, although I wished for a puppy and asked for one every Christmas, I never really expected to be getting one, and especially not with school starting the next week.

Here's how it all started. I came home from the five-and-ten-cent store loaded down with school supplies.

"Cookie! Just the person I want to see," said Daddy. Daddy is the only one who calls me Cookie. My real name is Olivia.

"In a minute." I dropped the heavy bag on the couch, glad the shopping was done. It's not that I don't like school, because I do. It's just this year was the first time I had done my back-to-school shopping without my best friend, Wei Ping.

When I went into the kitchen, Daddy was at the counter scraping fish and whistling. He leaned over and kissed my cheek. His mustache was tickly, but I never minded that. "Something wrong?"

I shook my head.

"Then why the long face?"

I shrugged. "I don't have a long face," I said. But I suppose he was right. I was hot, and inside I was feeling pretty icky.

"I have some news that'll make you smile." He grinned. His mustache seemed to stretch from one side of his face to the other. "Good news, Cookie."

"How good?" I've learned not to trust Daddy's good news.

"Well, I think it will make you very happy."

As always, I was hoping he was talking about a puppy. That would definitely make me happy. But with Daddy there was no telling. Daddy's *good news* announcements have fooled me before.

Once his good news was that his soufflé did not fall. Another time it was that he found the perfect name for the villain in the novel he was writing. The worst good news of all came yesterday when he told me I had gotten my first letter from Wei Ping. She used to be my best friend until she moved to California. That wasn't her fault, but did she have to love it out there so much? Did she have to meet a new girl the same day she moved who liked reading mystery stories and playing detective games just like we used to do? In that whole letter, she didn't say one word about missing me or about the gold charm I'd given her as a going-away present. She was one of the reasons I was feeling so miserable today.

"You sure this is going to make me *really* happy?" I finally asked as I flicked fish scales off my arm.

He winked at me. "Go get Drina. I'll tell you both at the same time." He kept on scraping the fish and whistling. Suddenly, I figured out what the song was. It was "How Much Is That Doggie in the Window?"

"Tell us *what?*" The back of my neck tingled.

"Go on now."

"Give me a hint," I begged.

Finally, he said, "All right, shweetheart, you got yourself one question," in his imitation of that old-time actor, Humphrey Bogart.

"Animal, vegetable, or mineral?" Animal, say, animal.

He whispered into my ear, "Animal."

A thousand goose bumps popped out all over me. I dashed into the room I shared with my sister, Drina. She is thirteen. She was gazing into the mirror, her arm stretched out, and a sick, teary-eyed expression on her face.

" 'O, find him! Give this ring to my true knight, and bid him come to take his last farewell.' " She took long strides across the room and stopped at her closet. She spun around. "What do you want?"

"Guess what I'm getting?"

She flipped through the pages of the play. "Who cares? Leave me alone. I'm rehearsing," she said importantly. The truth was, she wasn't rehearsing for anything. All summer long, she's been reading and studying Shakespeare's plays. She wants to get the leading role in her school play this fall. I bet a lot of girls in her school are better than she is. She doesn't even sound half good to me.

She cleared her throat, read some lines with her eyes cast toward the ceiling.

I went up to her and said above her speech, "Daddy is getting me a puppy."

She stopped, put the palm of her hand on my forehead.

I knocked her hand away. "What do you think you're doing?"

"Seeing how sick you really are."

"I am not sick."

"Use your head. Who's going to take care of a puppy?"

"Daddy must have it figured out. Anyway, he sent me in here to get you so he could tell us the news." I stuck out my tongue. "So there."

"Imbecile," she said, and pushed me down on the bed. But I bounced back up and trailed after her into the kitchen, where Daddy was still whistling that song.

Daddy slit open one of the fish and pulled out some pinkish, slimy guts.

"Sick," moaned Drina. "Do we have to eat fish every Friday?"

He started his once-a-week lecture on how nutritious fish is, low in fat, high in protein, high in . . .

"We can talk about fish anytime," I said. "Tell Drina what you just told me." I folded my arms across my chest.

For a moment he looked puzzled. Then he said, "Oh, yeah."

He waved the knife in the air, a big smile on his face, and said, "My sabbatical came through."

"Sabbatical! What about the puppy?"

"What puppy?"

"*The* puppy. The one that's going to make me happy. You said animal. You were even whistling 'How Much Is That Doggie in the Window?' If that doesn't add up to a puppy . . ."

"I think you just flunked arithmetic," Drina said, and burst into giggles.

Daddy touched my face with his fishy, smelly hands. "I'm sorry I misled you. When I said animal, I meant me."

Boy, that was sneaky. Worse than sneaky. It was downright mean. How did he think his sabbatical would make me happy? Sure, I loved that he was home all summer even if he did spend most of the time writing. Now that he'd be home all year, the house wouldn't be empty when I got home from school. That part was nice.

In a way, his sabbatical was good news, but a puppy would have been much better. Just then I got an idea. Why couldn't I still get a puppy?

"Daddy, now that you'll be home, I can get a puppy. I mean, before, nobody was, and it wouldn't've been fair. But now . . ."

Before Daddy could answer, big-mouth Drina blurted out, "Is that all you can think about—a dog? Daddy is trying to create the next *Gone With the Wind* or *Roots* or something. You want him to paper-train a dumb dog? You better remember what Ma said. We have to support each other. Support." She tugged my ear. "All for one and one for all."

"Lay off, Drina," said Daddy. He pulled the fish meat from the skeleton and placed the fillet on the waxed paper.

"I'm only trying to help," she grumbled.

"Then go and practice Juliet's speech in Act II, Scene 2."

" 'O Romeo, Romeo! . . .' I thought I said it perfectly already."

"No, needs more practice." He winked at her. "I'll help you in a bit. Go on."

When Drina was gone, Daddy looked down at me. I sniffed and wiped my nose on my arm. "I'm sorry you guessed wrong, Cookie. Sorry about the dog."

"But why?"

"For one thing, I won't have time to care for a puppy. But there's a more important reason why you can't get a puppy just now."

"I've tried so hard. I hang up my clothes. I do all my chores without you telling me to. I change my socks every single day, even on Saturday."

"You deserve a dog. I feel sure you'd take care of it, see to its needs, and give it lots of love."

"So, what's the problem?"

"Money. We'll be living off Mama's salary mostly. A puppy is an expense we can't afford."

"When can we afford it?"

He sighed. "I wish I could give you a definite answer, Cookie. But I can't." He picked a fish scale from my hair and flicked it into the sink. "Don't be too angry with me. Okay?"

Although I didn't answer right away, I understood everything he said about money and being so busy with rewriting his novel. If we could afford a dog, he'd buy me one. I knew that. I hugged him around his waist, feeling his heart thump against my face.

"I'm glad you got a whole year to write. I hope your book is a best seller and you get on the 'Today' show." He gave me a squeeze. "And I'm glad you'll be here when I get home from school. And I'm not mad either."

"I knew you'd understand."

I went and got my school supplies and started putting paper and indexes into my new looseleaf. I wished school were starting right that minute. If it were, I would be so busy making new friends, I wouldn't have time to think about how much I still wanted a puppy.

2 🐾

It was Sunday evening. School was starting tomorrow, and Ma was pinning up a hem on me. Although Daddy takes care of the cooking and cleaning, Ma does all the sewing and mending.

Usually, I'm happy about getting ready for the first day, but I was hating everything today. Especially this skirt and standing up on this stool.

"Done yet?" I asked, looking down. Half of the skirt was still hanging below my knees.

"Ten minutes more," Ma said. "And unless you want a crooked hem, hold still."

"I don't want to wear this skirt. Period."

"According to the saleslady, this is the latest style. All fifth-grade girls will be wearing pleats."

"She took a poll of every fifth grader in the city?"

"Now, that's silly," Ma said, tugging at the skirt. The

red checks were so big, they made me dizzy. Just before she finished pinning, the telephone rang.

I jumped down. "It's for me."

Drina grabbed the phone first. "Who'd be calling you?" She said, "Hello," then dragged the phone into the coat closet and shut the door. I got back on the stool.

When Drina came out, she said, "Lisa Peters, Felicia, Markie, and I are meeting at Carmen's house in the morning. Is that okay?"

"Yes," said Ma. She gave my skirt a final tug. "All done."

Later, the telephone rang again. It was for Ma this time. I put the sewing things away for her while she talked.

Daddy turned on "60 Minutes" and was filling his pipe. I sat next to him pretending to be interested in the show. I was thinking how lonely it had been since Wei Ping moved away. When the telephone rang a third time and it was for Drina again, Daddy asked, "Expecting a call?"

"Sort of," I said. I'd be in trouble if he asked whom I expected to call me, because the answer would be—nobody. But I had an idea. As soon as Drina finished, I called up Nilda Ramos, but she wasn't home. Then I called Helen.

Helen said, "Faye and I take the school bus. See you in school."

I was getting discouraged, but I didn't give up. I called Roxie Higgins. She had a voice that sounded like her nose was stuffed with cotton all the time. "I'm meeting Tawana at school. She's always late."

"What about Vicky?"

"What about her?"

"Never mind. Hey, what you wearing tomorrow?"

"Jeans, what else? That's what everybody's wearing. Aren't you? Dressing up is for babies."

I glanced over at Ma. She was already hemming the skirt. No one else was wearing pleats. Me neither. I didn't care what that saleslady said.

"I got to ask my mother," I said.

"Your mother!" She screamed into my ear. "Your mother still tells you what to wear?"

"No. Does yours?"

"Are you kidding? Look, I got to go."

How was I going to get out of it now? Ma was set on me wearing that dumb skirt and velveteen vest. If Wei Ping were going to be there, wearing a pleated skirt and vest, I wouldn't mind. I didn't want to look any different from everybody else. They wouldn't talk to me for sure, thinking I was too babyish to wear jeans the first day of school or just plain stuck up.

Daddy's arm was around Ma while she hemmed the skirt. Drina sat in the recliner, her legs propped up on the ottoman. She'd just finished painting every other toenail a different shade of red and was letting them dry. I was just about to do my evening chores. But I stood at the doorway to the living room. My heart pounded. Butterflies fluttered around inside me as I was about to tell Ma I was definitely not wearing that skirt. The words wouldn't come out. Ma laughed at something on the TV. Then her eyes locked into mine.

"Something wrong, Olivia?" she asked.

I shook my head.

"Sure?"

I nodded.

"Then stop moping around like a mummy," said

Drina. Daddy gave her a stern look, but that didn't stop Drina. "Ever since Wei Ping moved away, she's acted like she lost her one and only friend."

"Make her shut up," I said. She did, but Daddy gave me a sad look. He believed her. I hated Drina for that. True or not, there are some things no one wants their parents to know about them. "She's always talking about things she doesn't know anything about," I said. I turned and went into the kitchen to get the garbage.

As I was going out the front door, I heard Drina say, " 'You can fool some of the people some of the time, but you can't fool all the people all the time.' "

Such a know-it-all! I stomped down the hall to the compactor room. Just as I was about to shove the garbage down the chute, the door burst open. I was scared. I jumped and dropped the bag. Garbage splattered all over the floor.

A boy stood looking down at the mess, his mouth hanging open. I felt like stuffing garbage down his throat.

"Don't just stand there."

"I d-d-d-didn't m-m-m-mean . . ." He stamped his foot.

I pointed. "It was your fault. You clean it up."

I was shocked at what happened next. The boy got down on his knees and started shoving garbage into the bag with his hands! In my whole life no one ever obeyed me except for dogs. Pretending to toss a bone down the hall, I yelled, "Fetch!"

He started to run, stopped, then giggled. He bent down to finish.

I handed him an empty frozen food package. "Here. Use this."

While he raked up the rest of the garbage, he kept on

saying how sorry he was. He was the sorriest boy I'd ever met. Boy, did he look it! He had a flat head like someone sat on it when he was a baby. He wore thick glasses that kept falling down on his nose. His ears stuck out, and he wore beige and brown suede shoes that were big enough for a giant's feet.

"All right, already. Apology accepted. Nice knowing you," I said, and started back to my apartment.

He followed me. "I s-s-s-spoke th-th-th-this morn—" He stamped his foot again. It sounded like he was stomping out the giant ant from Mars.

I made like I was pulling the word from his mouth. "Come on. You can do it."

For some reason that made him smile. Then he said slowly, "I spoke to you this morning."

I clapped my hands. "Tell me, what planet you from?"

He broke into giggles.

"I mean," I said, shouting above his giggles, "are you from around here or what?"

That question was a mistake. Ask this kid one tiny question, and he gives you his whole life story. As if I should be interested. He told me he stuttered only when he was nervous. I clapped again, but he went on. He was going on ten like me and an only child like I wish I were. His name is Jeffrey Dingle. His parents are divorced. He was living with his father. When his father's job made him travel, he had to come and live with his aunt.

"You mean your aunt is Mrs. Dingle, the landlady?"

"You know her?" he asked, surprised.

"Well of course I know her. Mrs. Dingle owns this whole building plus the two stores downstairs. Good Stuff/Old Stuff belongs to my good, old friend, Mr. G. There's Connie's Bakery next door. She makes the best cookies in the world."

"What's your favorite kind?" he asked.

Before I could answer, Pearl came running up the hall, barking. She was loose again! Pearl is Mrs. Dingle's miniature poodle and runs away whenever she gets the chance, like if someone leaves the front door open. But Pearl either comes back home on her own or I find her and bring her back. Jeffrey Dingle didn't know all that. He got nervous and chased Pearl all around the hall, but he couldn't catch her.

"Pearl," I said in a stern voice, holding my right hand up. "Stay!" I kept pushing my right palm at her and commanding her to "Stay!" She finally stopped. "Sit." She did. "Good girl." I stroked her curly, cream-colored fur. "See how easy it is."

"Wow," he said, like I'd performed some kind of miracle. "Where'd you learn that?"

"Books."

"What's your favorite?" he asked eagerly.

I gathered Pearl into my arms. "You're a naughty dog." She nibbled my finger, but it didn't hurt one bit. In fact, it felt good. Even though Pearl did not belong to me, I loved her just like I loved Mr. G's dog, Killer. But not as much as I would love a dog of my very own.

I was curling Pearl's hair around my fingers when Jeffrey Dingle asked me a second time, "What's your favorite book?"

I knew he never heard of it let alone read it, but I told him just the same. "*The Double Trick Caper.* I read it *five* times. But I don't suppose you ever heard of it."

His eyes were as bright as light bulbs. "Heard of it! I read it five times too. It's *my* all-time favorite." He grinned.

I didn't know what to say or do. So I gave him my blankest stare.

"What other books you like?" he said.

"Uh . . ." I felt kind of funny inside, like one tiny butterfly was fluttering around inside me from my toes up to my ears. I gave Pearl back to him. "You better take her home now."

Pearl wiggled right out of his arms. She took off down the hall again, yipping and yapping. Jeffrey Dingle chased her, stumbling over his funny shoes. Just as he got close enough to catch her, Pearl wagged her tail, barked, then scampered away. It was a sight to see, like watching a speeded-up cartoon. Then they disappeared up the stairs. I laughed so hard my side ached.

That Jeffrey Dingle was a strange person (even if his favorite book is my favorite too). That night when I said my prayers, the last thing I said was "Please, God, don't let me ever see him again."

3 🐾

The next day was bright and sunny, the way the first day of school is supposed to be. Drina was dressed long before me. She looked almost grown-up in her pantsuit. She claimed it was the latest style for all eighth-grade girls. I wondered how people can claim to know those things. It makes no sense to me. Like wearing old clothes the first day of school made no sense either. But if that's how everybody else was dressing, I was not going to be the odd one. Somehow I had to get out of the house without them seeing me in faded jeans and my orange T-shirt that said, *Look at me. I'm the greatest.*

Drina was standing at the mirror rubbing clear lipgloss on her lips. Clear is the only color Ma lets her wear. I don't see why she even bothers. Her lips just look greasy.

I sat on the bed, still in my underwear, waiting for Drina to leave the room. Instead, she sat down beside me smelling like she'd bathed in her eau de cologne.

"What's wrong?" she asked.

I pursed my lips, not wanting to talk to her or anybody else about it.

"Come on, out with it. What's the problem?"

"Who said I had a problem, know-it-all?"

"You have that sick-rat expression again."

I slid away from her. "Go away and leave me alone."

She shrugged her shoulders and got up. But just as she was going out the door, she stopped, then turned around. She looked at me, then at the outfit hanging on the closet door, and broke out into giggles.

When she was gone, I shoved the skirt, blouse, and vest back into the closet. If I wore them, all the girls would laugh at me just like Drina had. I was not going to let that happen. I was going to wear exactly what Roxie said everyone else was wearing.

So I wiggled into the jeans and pulled the shirt over my head.

Next, I combed out my bangs and fastened barrettes to the tips of my braids. Looking myself over carefully in the mirror, I decided I liked what I saw. And I was going to stand up to Ma and Daddy no matter what. I put my books and pencils into my book bag and marched out of my room. From the living room, I heard their laughter and talking over the clinking of forks against plates. Suddenly, my insides were jiggling loose. My nerve was fizzling away. But I had to do it. I tiptoed to the dining room door. Maybe I'd just slide into my seat and they wouldn't notice me. Daddy was showing Ma a news article. She looked very intense, with her eyebrows drawn together. I tiptoed in. They were still involved in the article. Drina looked up. Her eyes popped out.

"Goodness. Look at you!"

Ma and Daddy both looked up. They were tongue-tied. They just stared at me for a long time. I sat down and dumped corn flakes into my bowl.

Ma finally spoke. "Didn't you see the outfit?"

"Yes, but . . ."

"Come on, Olivia, you can't go like that."

"But . . . but . . . if I change now, my corn flakes will get soggy." I poured the milk in a hurry.

Drina burst out laughing. Daddy gave her a look that shut her up.

"Well?" Ma asked.

"It's not fair."

"Here we go again," Drina said.

"What's not fair?" Ma asked.

"Drina gets to pick her clothes. Why not me?"

"I'm a sensible person," Drina said. "Besides, *I* have taste. *I'd* be too ashamed to show myself in public dressed like that."

"And I hate arguments at eight fifteen in the morning," said Daddy.

Ma glanced at the clock on the wall. "I'm going to be late." She gulped down the last of her coffee, grabbed her briefcase and newspaper. "Alex, will you take care of this?" Meaning me. Daddy told Ma not to worry.

As soon as Ma was gone, I said to him, "I'm ten years old. Practically."

"I know how old you are." He was writing something down on a long, yellow pad. Nowadays he always kept a pad and pencil near him.

"Well, isn't that old enough to pick out my own clothes?"

He scrunched up his face. "You really want to go like that?"

"I really do."

"Then it's settled." He winked at me. I winked back.

I finished my breakfast and left. I stopped off at Good Stuff/Old Stuff as usual to say hi to Mr. G. He wasn't really open yet, but he opened the door for me.

He looked me up and down. "Thought this was the first day of school."

"It is."

"And you going like that?"

"So, what about it?" I asked.

He hunched his shoulders. "Nothing, I reckon. Each and everyone to his own."

"I'll come by later," I told him, and headed for school. On the way I noticed lots of kids all dressed up. Now I was wondering if wearing these ratty old clothes was right. What worried me more was that almost everyone was walking in groups or pairs. From what I could see, I was the only one all alone. I hurried into the yard and got myself mixed in with a crowd of kids going into the building.

Everyone I passed in the halls was dressed in crisp, new clothes that still had a just store-bought smell. I felt like a jerk. But then I got to my room. I was shocked to see the girls were dressed in jeans and T-shirts like me. Roxie was right after all. What a relief! I said hi to everyone. They said hi back and wanted to know if I'd heard from Wei Ping.

"Not yet," I said. I didn't want to tell them how happy she was. "Hi," I said to Vicky. She was the most popular girl in the school, practically. She knew all the latest dances and was the best double-dutch jumper.

"Hi," she said. "I like your jeans."

"Yours too," I said, and started to slide into the seat next to hers.

But she put her hand over it. "I'm saving it for Roxie. Sit there." She tapped the seat in front of her.

Of all the kids in the room, I was the only one sitting alone. I'd never sat alone before. I kept shifting around, feeling everyone's eyes on me.

After the teacher, Ms. Leslie, greeted us and told us about all the work we'd be doing this year, she said, "I'm sure you're aware we lost one student this year. But we're getting a new one."

"Boy or girl?" I asked, crossing my fingers.

"God, please let it be a boy," said Noel—he folded his hands as if he were praying—"who can play center field."

"Boy or girl," said Ms. Leslie, "we need a buddy."

"Yick." Noel pinched his nose.

"Oh, no," someone else moaned.

Every kid coming into West Side Free School had to have a buddy. The buddy showed her around the school and helped her out whenever she needed help. The buddy system lasted for one week. If the kid was a creep, that was five days of torture. But it could turn out to be your new best friend.

"Any volunteers?" Ms. Leslie asked.

No one said a word. I had an idea. It was likely the new kid would be a girl since the class had eleven boys and only seven girls. I took a chance and raised my hand.

Vicky tapped me on the shoulder. "That was a dumb thing to do."

"Says who?"

She nodded her head toward the door. "Look for yourself."

4 🐾

The new kid was not a girl, not even a
creepy one. It was Jeffrey Dingle. I'd never had such bad
luck in all my life! When Ms. Leslie explained that I was
his buddy, he put on a big grin. That wasn't so bad. It's
what he did next that made me want to die.

"She's my buddy already," he said. The class giggled,
and I felt like a dope. Vicky tapped me on the shoulder
and wiggled her eyebrows up and down. Brother! I really got myself into a mess this time, and there was no
getting out of it.

"Don't you want a boy to be your buddy?" I asked.

"You're fine," he said.

Vicky and Roxie burst into laughter. Helen leaned
over and whispered something.

It was the way Jeffrey Dingle acted that made everyone feel funny. For example, most boys, like Noel

or Jorge, yanked my braids and stuck out a foot when I walked by. Noel would offer me a stick of gum, then stuff it into his own mouth just as I reached for it.

Not Jeffrey Dingle! I tripped over his foot, and he made a big deal about saying he was sorry. He even picked up the papers I'd been carrying. I was handing out the social studies books and one dropped. I expected Jeffrey to send it skidding across the room. That's what Noel would have done. But Jeffrey picked it up, dusted it off, and even offered to help me. All the girls started giggling. I was so embarrassed.

Being a buddy did not include walking to and from school together. But he was waiting for me that day and every day for the rest of the week.

"He must be up to something," Vicky said on Friday.

"Must be," I said, eyeing him as he talked to Ms. Leslie about his reading homework.

When he returned to his seat, I edged to the other side of mine and hung off the edge all morning. He offered me a stick of Juicy Fruit gum. I shook my head. I couldn't take him much longer. But then I remembered it was Friday. After today, he had no reason to hang around me.

On my way to school the next Monday morning, he was waiting for me downstairs in the lobby. While we walked, he kept talking and I hummed. A lot of people were staring at us. I wondered if they thought he was my boyfriend or something. I wanted him to go away and leave me alone, but for some reason I couldn't tell him.

Jeffrey kept hanging around me. The kids giggled,

snickered, and cracked jokes about us. Someone even drew a heart on the board one day and put O. L. LOVES J. D. inside the heart with an arrow running through it. I could have died on the spot.

That wasn't the worst of it. During recess I was sitting on the stone ledge waiting for a turn to jump into the rope. Who should sit beside me but Jeffrey Dingle. I inched over and pretended he did not exist.

Before long Jeffrey started up. "Want to play handball or something?"

"No."

"Tag?"

"Leave me alone." I cupped my chin in my hands and wondered when the girls were going to ask me to jump.

"Later then?"

I gave him my meanest look. *"N-O."*

"How come?"

"Because at this very moment, I am conducting a very important investigation."

His eyes lit up. "Then let's play detective. I love detective games."

"This is real stuff," I said. "No room for amateurs."

Jeffrey was like a hungry mosquito, always buzzing around. And like a mosquito, I'd have to squash him but good. It happened at lunchtime.

I was on an errand when the lunch period started and was the last one in my class to get in line. It was spaghetti day. The place smelled of tomato sauce. I was starving, but the line was moving slowly. When I leaned over to see what was taking so long, I noticed the lunchroom lady passing out bowls of butterscotch pudding. My mouth watered, and my stomach growled.

When I finally reached the dessert end, the lunchroom lady started placing dishes of green Jell-O on each tray.

"What happened to the pudding?" I asked.

"All out," she said. She put the green Jell-O on my tray.

I gave it back to her. "I hate Jell-O, especially the green kind. You must have one butterscotch pudding. Somewhere."

"No more pudding. Take Jell-O or nothing."

When I paid for my lunch, I asked the cashier if I could get a discount since I didn't have dessert. She took my money and said, "Next."

Most of the kids were at the table already. Jeffrey slid in last across from Noel and Jorge. What was Jeffrey doing on the girls' side of the table?

He slid farther down. "Sit here," he said.

I sat down only because there was no place else to sit. Noel and Jorge began snickering. It seemed like all the other kids were holding back their laughter too.

As I dug into the spaghetti, Jeffrey put his bowl of pudding on my tray. "What do you think you're doing?" I asked.

"Why, Olivia, that's your engagement present," said Vicky.

Noel and Jorge cracked up, jabbing each other in the sides.

I was boiling mad and gave Jeffrey my meanest glare. "I don't want it. Take it back," I said. I refused to even touch the dish. Now I was sure something sneaky was going on, and that Noel and Jorge were in on it.

"I want you to have it," Jeffrey said, and he wasn't taking no for an answer.

That's when I figured it out. When we get a good

dessert like ice cream, some kids pretend they are being nice and offer you their Dixie cups. But when you pull up the lid, there's no ice cream inside. The cup is filled with mushed-up peas and potatoes.

"Go on, Olivia," said Noel.

"Scaredy-cat," hooted Jorge.

I grunted and turned up my nose at them. But I was secretly wondering what was under that pudding. A wad of chewed-up gum? A rubber spider? A *real* spider? I wasn't taking any chances. I'd make Jeffrey Dingle leave me alone once and for all. "If I don't feel like eating pudding, I don't have to eat it." In one great gesture, I dumped the bowl of pudding on top of Jeffrey's plate of spaghetti. "Here, you eat it."

It was dead quiet at the table. Every eye was on me now as I pulled the bowl up. "Ta da!"

I looked down at Jeffrey's plate, prepared for some horror. But I wasn't prepared for what I saw. There were no spiders or chewed-up gum at the bottom of the pudding dish. There was nothing but pudding. He hadn't tricked me at all!

Jeffrey's eyes drew up into thin, angry slits. His cheeks puffed up and he said, "I'll g-g-g-get you."

"Sock her now, Jeff, old boy," Noel called out, making fake punches at the air. Everyone started yelling, screaming, jumping up and down, and falling all over themselves laughing.

Jeffrey stood up slowly, his eyeglasses shining blankly. I wasn't staying there another second. I scrambled out of my seat, ran into the hallway, and flopped against the wall. The cool breeze felt good brushing against my face, but it didn't stop my heart from pounding.

"Not eating?" the principal asked on her way into the lunchroom.

I was starving, but I wasn't going back in there. I can never face them again, I thought. Not now. Not ever.

5 🐾

I could not go home either and face Daddy. I didn't want him finding out what a terrible thing I had done. There was only one place to go—Mr. G's. I watched him through the glass door of his store, then opened the door slowly so the bell would not ring. It rang anyway, but Mr. G was so busy reading his *Antique Dealer and Collector's Guide*, he didn't even notice me.

Killer padded to me. Killer is part German shepherd. I gave him a big hug. He rewarded me with a big, wet lick across my face. I tiptoed to the armchair and plunked down, with my legs swung across one arm. I kicked slowly against the chair, and picked at the gold threads.

I wish someone had told me going on ten was so terrible. Nothing has gone right since the day Wei Ping left. I won't ever stop missing her.

"Didn't hear you come in." Mr. G closed the book and put it back on the shelf. "School's out already?" He checked a small alarm clock on the shelf in back of him.

I pressed my lips together. I wasn't going to talk about it. I folded my arms and promised myself not to say a word.

"Stomach tells me it's 'round about lunchtime."

"I'm not hungry."

"I am. Get the door." He went into the back. I stayed where I was. The only way to stick to my word was to stay out of his sight. But when he called, I got up.

I've eaten with him often enough to know what to do. I hung the OUT TO LUNCH sign in the door window, then locked the door. I followed the smells of steamy vegetable soup to the back room, zigzagging my way in and around racks of antique clothes, stacks of chairs, tables and old paintings propped up against an old bookcase. I edged sideways through the chests of drawers and bureaus. Killer was so big, he had a tough time getting through the narrow aisles. I tell Mr. G that we should make the store neater. He says people expect to see clutter in an antique store.

I reached the back room, where Mr. G was filling the copper kettle with water. The room is like a small apartment. It has everything anyone could need: sink, table, chairs, even a rollaway bed. While Mr. G made the sandwiches, humming all the while, I got the table ready. I wiped it with a soft chamois cloth until the wood had a waxy shine. In the middle of the table I placed a straw basket filled with gourds of different shapes and sizes. Then, a place mat for each of us with a napkin. We worked quietly. We always did. In a few minutes, the table was decorated as if it were out of a magazine. Mr.

G had made finger sandwiches in bite-size triangles. He added chocolate chip cookies from Connie's Bakery next door, and a soup tureen filled with steamy, hot soup. No matter what the weather is, Mr. G makes soup. He ladled some into my bowl as I dumped myself into the chair opposite him.

"I told you I'm not hungry," I said, and pushed the bowl away, but that soup sure smelled good.

He broke a hunk of bread in two and dipped it down in the thick vegetable soup. "How was school this morning?" he asked, his mouth full of bread.

I lowered my head so as not to look into those gray eyes of his. Maybe I should have stayed away. Maybe Mr. G couldn't help me after all. I started to get up, but he reached for my hand.

"Something wrong?"

"Why you think something's wrong?" I asked.

"Just asked. You in some kind of trouble?"

Without answering, I sniffed and wiped my nose on my sleeve. He whipped out his big, plaid handkerchief.

"Blow your nose," he said.

"I'm not crying," I said, then blew hard into the handkerchief. "I just got a runny nose."

"I get those too every now and then." He stuffed the handkerchief back into his pocket when I gave it to him. "Now, sit down and eat. I bet you ain't had a thing since breakfast time."

"I bet you're wrong." I slid back into the chair, but didn't touch the soup. My stomach felt like it had knotted itself, then shriveled up. After a while, I said, "Want to hear a sad story?"

"Not especially," he said, and slurped soup.

"Listen anyway," I said, and then went on to tell him

everything that happened with Jeffrey and me since the first day of school. After it was all over, I sniffled a bit.

"Say something," I said.

"Girl, here lately, every time I see you, you got trouble coming out of your eyeballs." He chuckled.

I could see nothing funny about what happened today. I had not one real friend. How could even Jeffrey be friends with a person who ruined his lunch? Trouble coming out of my eyeballs fit me perfectly.

"You said it!" I said.

"What I wouldn't give to have your kind of troubles."

"Take them. They're yours."

He chuckled again.

I clapped my hands and whistled for Killer to come. He obeyed and sat next to me while I stroked his soft, warm fur. He licked my hand, and I felt wanted, loved for the first time in a long while.

"This puts me in mind of when I was your age." Mr. G scratched his bristly chin.

"Huh? What?"

"My brother Bo was always stealing my thunder."

"What's that got to do with me?" I scratched Killer under his chin. He liked that a lot.

"Maybe nothing. It's just I used to feel cheated." His bullet gray eyes pierced me straight to the heart.

"Not me." I said real fast. "I don't feel the least bit cheated." Cheated. How did Mr. G know so much about my feelings? I kept on petting Killer as Mr. G talked.

"Bo was two years younger than me. Teacher's pet. Mama's pet. A passel of friends swarming around him. To top that, he could lick me in anything. You think you've got problems. I was the original problem kid." He poked himself in the chest.

"So, what about it?"

He scratched his chin again. "Well, I put on my thinkin' cap, got those gray cells a-workin'. And one day, Lord, if I didn't come up with a scheme to top 'em all." He smiled, and his mind seemed to be going back to that time long ago.

I shook his arm finally. "Go on. Tell me what you did."

He stuck his thumb in the air.

"You outtricked your brother! How?"

"Frog jumpin' contest. Mine was named Kingfish. Each and every day, I turned him loose in the barn and let him jump from one end to the other. Bo didn't bother with his frog. He just kept it in a box on the windowsill. That boy was that sure of himself."

"You beat him, right?" I pulled the bowl of soup to me and began eating while Mr. G talked.

"I won. But not how you think." He scratched his chin and chuckled. "The morning of the race, I filled an eyedropper with some of my daddy's best corn liquor."

"You got Bo's frog drunk?"

"You heard of that story 'The Tortoise and the Hare'? That gives you an idea of how slow Bo's frog was." Mr. G laughed so hard he ended up with a coughing fit.

"That poor frog."

He waggled his hand. "He wasn't hurt none. Just slowed down a bit."

"First of all, that was a sneaky thing to do." I giggled. "Second of all, how is that supposed to help me?"

"It just goes to show you can finagle a solution out of every problem."

"You know what mine's going to be? I'm going to walk to the edge of the world and jump off."

"Now, you're exaggerating, Libby Lou."

"Want to bet?" I asked. "That Jeffrey Dingle will never speak to me again. What's more, I bet he's laying a *real* trap for me now."

Mr. G shook his head from side to side. "There you go again, looking for trouble."

"Am not." I played with the soupspoon awhile, then said, "I'm even sorry about what I did."

He wiped his mouth and handed Killer some leftover bread, "Ain't you telling this to the wrong person?"

I hunched my shoulders and kept playing with the spoon.

"That boy could turn out to be a mighty good friend."

"Baloney. You know how boys are. Deep down, Jeffrey Dingle's no different, I bet." But I wasn't all that sure anymore, and something about Jeffrey kept nudging at me.

Mr. G patted my hand. We finished our lunch.

"Time to get back to school," he said when it was almost one o'clock. He walked me to the door, his hand on my shoulder.

Just as I was about to leave, Miss Connie, from the bakery, stormed inside. She waved a long envelope at Mr. G.

"This is going to be the end of me!" she shouted. "That Annabelle Dingle."

"What's she done now?" Mr. G asked.

"Look for yourself." She thrust the letter at Mr. G. "I knew this was coming. There's no sense in waiting. I'm going to do it now."

Mr. G raised his hand for her to slow down while he read the letter. He caught me peeking, and folded it up before I got a chance to read it.

"Sit down, Connie. Relax yourself."

"Relax!" She paced up and down. "How can I relax when I'm being destroyed?"

I whispered to Mr. G, "How's Jeffrey Dingle's aunt destroying Miss Connie?"

"Never you mind," he said. "You get back to school."

"I have to?" I was hoping he would say I could stay with him until three o'clock. Except for the time I had chicken pox, I've never been absent from school. I didn't want to be absent today, but I didn't want to go back either.

"You have to," he said.

"But when they all laugh at me— What then?"

"First off, walk in the room with your head held high, then pull your shoulders back." He straightened out his own shoulders.

"That's really going to help?" I asked doubtfully.

"Have I ever let you down?"

"Never. Okay then."

He added, "And have that talk with Jeffrey."

"I'm not going to promise, but maybe."

By the time I got to the classroom, everyone was doing their silent reading. I smoothed down my bangs and tucked in my shirt. Then, head up, shoulders pulled back, I walked into the room.

6 🐾

No one, not one single person, looked up! No one noticed me. I plopped down at my seat and took out my book. Now and then, I glanced over at Jeffrey when I thought he was looking at me. Only he never was. I thought of taking Mr. G's other advice too and apologizing to Jeffrey, but my nerve fizzled away. Besides, with my luck, I thought, he might tell me to get lost or drop dead or something terrible like that.

I dug into my work and pushed Jeffrey Dingle and everyone else out of my mind. It was hard, though, especially when Tawana giggled at something Helen said, or when Vicky whispered secrets to Roxie. I felt like I was in a tiny boat all alone drifting farther and farther out to sea.

One afternoon, everything changed. I took the long way home through the park. Every now and then, I turned around to make sure Jeffrey wasn't tagging behind me. He wasn't. I was all alone. I went down the slide once. That was no fun. Then I got on the swing. I just sat there like a lump because I can't pump myself and Wei Ping used to push me. I sat there awhile anyway, feeling the cool breeze brush against my cheeks. Suddenly, I saw a yellow Frisbee sail through the air. Then a big, gray sheep dog went chasing after it. I held my breath as he ran toward it. Just as the Frisbee was about to land, the dog caught it between his teeth. "Yaaaaayyy!" I screamed, and clapped for him.

Each time the dog caught the Frisbee, he ran back to his master, a lady in a fur jacket. They played over and over. I cheered, clapped, and giggled. I never had this much fun since . . . since . . . I didn't even want to think about it. I was having fun now and wasn't even playing.

What really surprised me was that the dog never ran away from the lady to chase squirrels or anything. The dog played on and on even though it must have been boring to chase the same Frisbee time and time again. But he did because he was a loyal and loving friend. Like Killer was to Mr. G. Like Pearl was to Mrs. Dingle and Jeffrey. A puppy. If only I had a puppy of my own, there would be something to love me and stay by my side. Mr. G was right. There is a solution to every problem. A puppy is my solution. Somehow, I had to make Daddy see it my way. I know I promised to wait, but I was desperate for a puppy now. Besides, how much can a puppy cost? I hurried home. All the way, I prayed Daddy would say yes. He just had to.

The door to Daddy's study was closed. Inside he was typing. Asking for a puppy was important enough to interrupt, I decided, and went inside. Crumpled-up papers were everywhere.

"Daddy?" He kept typing. I stood over him. "Daddy?"

"Please don't stand over me, Cookie," he said without stopping his typing. He typed so fast it was as if he were racing.

I plopped down in his swivel chair and spun 'round and 'round waiting for him to notice me.

"Daddy, this is very important," I said after waiting a long time. "A matter of life or death."

Tappity tappity tappity tap . . . tappity tappity tappity tap . . .

"Daddy!"

He stopped typing at last. "Can it wait till later?" he asked.

"It's about a puppy," I said, but he had already started typing again and wasn't listening to a word I said. So I left.

A while later, he called me back into the room. I was hoping we'd talk about getting me the puppy. He handed me another letter from Wei Ping. I lay across my bed and read it.

Dear Olivia,
    I still can't believe the sun shines almost all the time. It does. Every day I'm making more and more friends. But that's probably nothing compared to all your new friends. I want to know all about them.
    Any new kids in the class? Tell everybody hi for me.
                                        Love,
                                    Wei Ping
P.S. The necklace did not turn green. I never take it off except for when I take a bath because Mom makes me. Did you get a dog yet?
    Please write. I'm dying to know all the exciting things you're doing.

She'd have a long wait. Nothing was exciting in my life. I held Thomasina a long time, thinking about the fun I could be having. Oh, how I wished she were real right this minute! I stroked her furry ears and squeezed her pudgy body.

I heard Drina come in and shoved Thomasina back with all the other stuffed dolls and animals. All I needed was for Drina to make fun of me now. I got out my science book and tried to start an outline. Drina twirled and danced around the room, singing, " 'I feel pretty, oh, so pretty. . . .' " She dropped her books on her desk, then danced back out again.

A few moments later, she was back. This time no dancing, no singing. She plopped down on her bed.

"You won't believe what just happened. I tried to tell Daddy how I got the leading part in the play. He acted like I was telling him the weather or something. 'Uh huh, that's great.' Tappity, tappity, tap . . ." Then in a sulky, hurt kind of voice, she said, "It's not every day a person's daughter gets to be a star." She folded her arms across her chest and sat that way for a long time. Her feelings were hurt, and no doubt she was holding back tears too. But I didn't feel sorry for her, not one bit. After all, she was a star. What more did she want?

"I don't even think he was listening," she mumbled.

"What do you expect?" I asked. "It's not like you won the Academy Award or like you're in a *real* play on a *real* stage."

Her mouth dropped open, but not a sound came out. When she did speak, her words went through me like a razor. "You're jealous. One hundred percent jealous."

I put my face back in the book. "I am not jealous."

"What do you call it?"

I threw the book on the bed, and jumped up to leave. "Shut up," I yelled.

"Brilliant," she said as I slammed the door.

7 🐾

That night at dinner, Daddy came into the dining room balancing a huge platter up in the air with one hand. *"La pièce de résistance,"* he said. His apron had *Le Chef* written across it.

"Since when do you speak French?" Drina asked.

"One of my many secrets," he said in a sly voice, and winked.

I never knew he kept secrets either. He set the platter in the center of the table. It was piled with reddish brown rice. Mixed with the rice were hunks of chicken, red slivery things, and green peas.

"It looks delicious, honey," Ma said. For a change, she was home on time. It was like it used to be when we ate dinner together all the time.

"Arroz con pollo," Daddy announced as he served everyone.

"What's that mean?" I picked the slivery things out of my plate.

"Spanish for chicken with rice."

"It's a masterpiece, Alex," said Ma after tasting it.

"To be perfectly honest," Daddy said, "the rice was instant, the pimentos and peas came from a can. The butcher even cut up the chicken for me. I just mushed everything together and *Voilà! Arroz con pollo.* What do you think, Drina?"

"It's good." But she was only pushing food from one side of her plate to the other. She wasn't eating a thing.

"I hope so," he said. "It's in your honor." He winked at her.

"My? . . . Oh, Daddy!" She jumped up and hugged him. He kissed her and held her close.

"What's going on?" Ma asked.

With his arm around Drina's waist, Daddy said, "Our Drina landed the starring role in the school play."

"We're doing *West Side Story*, and I'm playing Maria." Now, Ma was hugging and kissing Drina and saying how proud she was of her. Tears streamed down Drina's face, and Daddy dabbed them off with his napkin.

"Hey, want to hear what happened to me today?" I asked, but they were paying attention to Drina, the star.

"I was so nervous," she began, and clutched her chest in an overdramatic gesture. "I can't put on a Spanish accent, and I told that to Mr. Farley. And he said it was all right. The play won't be about a Puerto Rican gang against a white gang. The Sharks and Jets will be just two feuding gangs, period."

"Then that *West Side Story* is a fake," I said.

"For your information, smarty-pants, *West Side*

Story is based on *Romeo and Juliet*. That was about two feuding Italian families. It must be fate," she said dreamily. "Studying Juliet's part and now playing Maria." She sighed.

"How about a toast?" Daddy raised his lemonade glass. Our glasses clinked. All through dinner, Drina went on and on. They acted like I didn't even exist.

Toward the end of dinner, Daddy asked, "You had something to tell us, Cookie?" I shook my head no. It didn't matter now. I had figured out a way to get the puppy on my own.

Later, in my room, I opened the closet and pushed my clothes to one side. There it was. My old wooden toy chest. I rummaged through roller skates, broken dolls, a doctor's kit, and puzzles. Finally, I felt the sharp corners of the cigar box and pulled it out, careful not to make too much noise. I didn't want anyone asking any questions.

I brought the box to my bed. Mr. G had given it to me in third grade. He had showed me how to decoupage it by pasting on magazine pictures, then shellacking them so the box looked old and antique. He called it a rainy day box, a place to keep money for a rainy day.

When Mr. G first gave me the box plus a dollar bill inside, I told him it was a dumb idea. He laughed. "You just keep adding money to it. You'll be glad one day." He was right, as usual.

I counted out thirty-three dollars and five cents. I didn't even know I had that much. I was going to take every cent of it with me to the pet store and buy the softest, friendliest, most loving puppy in the world.

After school the next day, I headed downtown to the pet store. About halfway there, something strange happened. Someone was following me. I was sure of it. Each time I turned around, I thought I saw someone ducking between parked cars. Jeffrey, no doubt. He's not mad anymore. I got a terrific idea and ran to the subway. I flew down the stairs as a train rumbled into the station. I did not go through the turnstiles. I ducked down on the other side of the token booth. I could hear Jeffrey's heavy footsteps clumping down the stairs trying to catch up to me. I couldn't wait for him to jump on the train. What a joke on him!

But it was not Jeffrey at all. It was a grown man pushing through the turnstiles. Where was Jeffrey? I looked all around. Jeffrey was nowhere in sight. I went back upstairs. No Jeffrey. I could have sworn he was behind me. It looked like the joke was on me. Again.

I kicked a can down the block. It made such a hollow, empty sound. I finally kicked it into the gutter and hurried to the pet store.

From a block away, I saw the blue and white banner, PET PARADE, flapping in the air. When I went inside, stinky animal smells mixed with ammonia took my breath away. After a while, I got used to the smell.

The store was crammed with dog and cat supplies— food, shampoo, beds, pillows, toys, scratching posts. Along one wall were the cages of dogs stacked one on top of the other. A man came out of the back. He wore a rubber apron, and his face was thin and pinched looking.

"Yeah, what do you want?"

"A puppy." I took off my shoe and pulled the money out of my sock. "See, I have money."

He just looked at me.

"I never thought about a special breed," I said, feeling a little bit nervous for some reason. Suddenly I thought that maybe he wouldn't sell me a dog. He had all kinds—shepherds, cocker spaniels, collies, and some I did not recognize.

"No fooling?" he said in a bored way.

"But I don't want a puppy that needs hours at a dog parlor. It can't shed a lot of hair either. It has to have good manners so I can train it easily. Another thing, it can't be too big. I live in an apartment."

He snorted. "You want a short-haired dog, hearty, and medium sized."

"Right!"

"I got a beagle." I followed him to the back of the store, whisking my hand along the row of metal leashes. He gave me a grumpy look. So I stopped.

In a cage off to the corner was a black and white beagle with brown markings around the face and ears. It was curled up into a silky, shiny ball. Its head rested on the edge of its food dish.

"It's a female," he said.

My heart thumped. I could hardly speak. I knew she was perfect, just what I wanted. I tapped on the window of her cage. Nothing happened. I tapped again, a third time, and then her eyes slid open. They were the biggest, brownest eyes I'd ever seen.

"I'll take her." I held out my money to him.

"She'll cost you two bills."

"That's all?" I'd have enough change to get a leash, collar, some grooming supplies. This was turning out better than I thought.

"Two bills means two hundred dollars." He looked me dead in the eye. "Plus tax."

"I don't have that much money."

He waved. "Good-bye."

"But you acted like I had enough."

He hunched his shoulders. "You ever need a good laugh?"

"No."

"Okay, I'm sorry." He blocked his face with his arms. "No, kid, I mean it. If I could help, I would. Dogs are expensive."

"Isn't there something cheaper?" I looked around and pointed to a scraggly haired white puppy. "That must be cheap."

"You for real, kid? *That* is one of my best pedigreed poodles. It'll run you . . ." He put up his hand, spreading his five fingers.

"Five hundred dollars?" I gulped. "It doesn't even look like a poodle," I said, picturing Pearl's neatly clipped fur.

"The beagle is the cheapest I got. Two hundred dollars. She's five months, a little too old for most people. If no one buys her, I'm sending her back to the kennel."

"Two hundred dollars, huh? Well, this is thirty-three dollars and five cents. Let me put a deposit down. Then I'll owe you . . ."

"Too much." He walked back to the front of the store.

"Why not? Department stores let you put things on layaway. Why not a puppy?"

"Because. That's why not."

"What kind of reason is that? I promise I'll pay you five dollars each week and in the meantime you get to keep the puppy."

"Look, kid, why don't you go up to the ASPCA?"

"I saw their dogs. We went on a class trip in third grade. Most of their dogs are fully grown. I want a puppy like that beagle. She's just right. She's every-thing I want. So you got to say yes."

After a long moment, he pulled a toothpick from be-hind his ear and began picking his teeth. "I tell you what."

"Anything. Anything. Just name it."

"She'll run you two hundred sixteen dollars and fifty cents. Now you put the thirty-three dollars down. Bring the rest next Friday by closing time." He pointed to the sign on the wall.

"Next Friday? But I can't have that much money by then. That's only a week away."

He threw up his arms.

"If . . . if I don't get all the money by then?"

"Don't worry, you'll get your deposit back. Every cent. And she goes back to the kennel. Fair enough?"

"That's not fair at all."

"Take it or leave it."

I gave him the money. He gave me a receipt.

"Now can I hold her?" I asked.

When the pet store man opened the beagle's cage, she scrambled to her feet. A million butterflies batted around inside me as he put the puppy into my arms.

My heart pounded. My knees wobbled. She was kind of heavy. I was scared I might drop her, but I didn't. I held her closer to my chest. Her black and white fur felt as smooth as satin. The brown parts on her ears and face were velvety soft. She was trembling.

"We call her Cleopatra," he said. "You can change her name if you buy her."

"Cleopatra?" She looked up at me like she under-stood. Her eyes were wet and sparkling. "Such a long name for a puppy. Cleo is better."

"She's named after that queen of Egypt. Don't suppose you know anything about her."

"My sister played Cleopatra in the school play last year," I announced proudly. It's not that I enjoy making a fuss over Drina. Enough people do that already. But I hated the pet store man to think I was an idiot. I went on about Cleopatra. "And all the Romans fell under her spell."

"Yeah," he grumbled, and took Cleo away from me.

"I'm not through holding her." I reached for her, but he locked her back in the cage.

"See why we call her Cleopatra?" he said, laughing.

Someone else came into the store, and he left me alone with Cleo's cage.

Cleo scratched at the window. I scratched the window too, but I couldn't feel anything but the coldness of glass. "I'll be back, Cleo. Wait and see."

8 🐾

One hundred and eighty-three dollars and forty-five cents! That was a fortune. Where was I going to get that much money? The first thing that came to my mind was to get a job. On the way home, I tried every store I came to, but I was either laughed at or told to get lost.

Then I headed for Connie's Bakery, thinking there I could earn some money and all the free cookies I could eat. When I reached the bakery, the door was locked. The lights were on and Miss Connie was nowhere in sight. That was odd for the middle of the afternoon.

I found her in Mr. G's store. When she saw me standing there, she cleared her throat and said, "Don't worry. I'll find a way. I'll be talking to you, Sam." She left before I could ask her for a job.

Mr. G nodded his head and got real busy spraying Windex on the counter. "How did school go today?"

"It went." Before he started asking me a bunch of questions, I blurted out what was on my mind. "Mr. G, I need a job, a real job that pays money. I'll work real hard. I promise."

"A job, for what?"

"A secret. So you know I can't tell."

He stuffed his hands in his pockets and rocked back and forth on his heels. "Now, I'm real good at keeping secrets."

I figured I could trust him not to tell anyone. He nodded while I told him about Cleo. "So you found yourself a puppy. Mmm! She sounds like a gem. What kind of work you want to do?"

I often swept for him, dusted, put on price tags, and rang up sales. Any of those would do, but Mr. G suggested I walk Killer for him. Up until now, he was the only one who walked Killer.

"You sure? You mean it?"

"You're gonna need the practice," he said.

I hugged him. "You won't be sorry. I'm going to give Killer lots of exercise."

"Let's talk finance."

"You mean how much you're going to pay me?"

"If I could, I'd buy you the puppy myself. As it is . . . well, never mind. How much do you think you need?"

For a long time, Mr. G's business has been bad. As much as I wanted this puppy, I did not want him to go broke on account of me. "How about two dollars a week?"

"I'll make it five. I'll see what else I can finagle."

I hugged him again. "I knew I could count on you." He patted my back, and his hands were trembling.

Five dollars wasn't a lot, but it was the beginning. I

was sure I'd make enough money because Saturday evening I got another great idea. I couldn't put it into action until the next morning.

It wasn't even eight o'clock when I crawled out of bed the next day. No one was up yet. I tiptoed into the kitchen. Very quietly, I took two frying pans and the baking dish out of the cabinet and started making breakfast—eggs, sausages, and hot Danish. This had to work! When I had set the table and made the coffee, Ma came into the dining room. She was wearing her tight designer jeans.

"The good tablecloth and the crystal goblets for breakfast? If you break one . . ."

"I won't, Ma. I won't. Now, just sit down. I fixed everything." I pulled out Ma's chair.

"Alex, you better come in here," she called.

Daddy stumbled in, his bathrobe drooping off his shoulders, his eyes half closed. But when he saw the table set with good china, a vase of dried wild flowers that I had sprayed with Drina's perfume, and the Sunday *Times* on the table by the window, he flipped too. I put the Business section by Ma's place and the Book Review by Daddy's. I poured their juice into the crystal goblets.

"This is fresh squeezed," I boasted.

"Is that a hint?" Daddy asked. He only makes the frozen kind.

"Alex," Ma teased. Then they made goo-goo eyes at each other.

When they finished their juice, I served their coffee, making sure they knew it was freshly perked with freshly ground beans. "And it's strong, just the way you like it."

Drina came in when I was about to serve eggs and sausage. Her short, curly hair was swept to one side with a barrette. She took one look at everything, then at me, and said, "What's up?"

"Sit down, Drina, and enjoy," Ma said.

Drina slid into her chair hesitantly. " 'Something is rotten in the state of Denmark,' " she quoted from Shakespeare.

"It's not the Danish," said Daddy with his mouth full.

"Don't be so suspicious. Now, everybody, eat," said Ma.

"No way." Drina got a box of corn flakes from the cabinet. She was going to spoil everything.

When breakfast was over, Daddy got up with his coffee cup. "I'll finish this inside. Got some work to do."

"Me too," Ma said, and started to get up too.

"Wait a minute. I didn't . . ."

"Ah-ha! The plot thickens," said Drina.

"Sit down, Ma, Daddy."

"What did I tell you?" Drina folded her arms, looking smug.

"Make her shut up."

"Shut up, Drina," Daddy said jokingly. "All right, Cookie. What gives?"

"Well, Daddy, I need some money."

He pulled out his billfold and gave me my allowance. "You didn't have to do all this for . . ." He pressed two dollars and fifty cents into my hand.

"I didn't. . . . See, I need more than this. Can I have an advance on my allowance?"

"Sure." Daddy started to pull out a five-dollar bill. "How much? A week? Two weeks?"

"Fifty-two weeks."

He closed his wallet and put it back into his pocket.

"That's a whole year," Ma said. "You realize that's one hundred and thirty dollars?" Why did Ma have to be so fast with numbers?

I nodded. "But I need it."

"Why?" Ma, Daddy, and Drina asked at the same time.

I couldn't tell them. I couldn't tell them all the reasons I wanted a dog and how a dog would solve all my problems.

"Can't you just trust me?"

"That's a whole lot of trust," Daddy said. "One hundred and thirty dollars worth." He took a long gulp of coffee and set the cup down. He winked at me. "A terrific breakfast just the same." He went into his study.

I wanted to scream at him.

"Ma?"

Ma started clearing the table. "You heard your father."

"It's something for all of us, not just for me."

"It's too much money for a little girl."

She didn't know. She didn't know anything about me anymore. She was hardly ever home. It was not too much money for me. Somehow, I was going to get enough money to buy Cleo. I wouldn't tell them anything. I'd just bring her home and that would be that. In the meantime, I had to find a way to get the money. It looked hopeless.

Then a miracle happened on Thursday. I was on my way to school. As I was going out of the apartment lobby, Jeffrey Dingle was coming in. That was strange since school was just about ready to start. I didn't care why he was going the wrong way. I just tried to avoid him in case this was the day he decided to get even with me for putting the butterscotch pudding on his spaghetti. I jumped out of the way, but I was too late. He bumped into me, and his arms shot up. I ducked. He had a handful of blue papers. He didn't sock me. He didn't even notice me! I turned and went back inside to see what he was up to.

Jeffrey stood in front of the bulletin board, and I stood behind him, not too close. He tacked up one of his blue sheets of paper, then went to the elevator.

REWARD
for the return of a
LOST DOG
miniature poodle, cream
color, pink barrettes,
answers to name of
PEARL
call: 815-6902
OWNER HEARTBROKEN!

What kind of joke was that! Pearl! Lost? My common sense told me it was a big lie. I giggled.

He turned around. "Well? What's so funny?"

"That." I pointed to the sign. "What fool's going to fall for that?"

"P-P-P-Pearl's r-r-r-really . . . She's gone."

"Gone? I don't believe it."

He punched the elevator button. "I don't care whether you believe me or not."

"It's not a trick to make me look stupid?"

"I don't have to th-th-th-think up anything to make you look stupid."

"I'll ignore that."

The elevator came. I followed him inside.

"What you going to do with all those signs?" I asked.

"Put them up like I did the others." He stared up at the indicator buttons.

"Where?"

"Everywhere. Store windows, lampposts."

"For the whole, entire world to see?" Pearl must really be lost. Suddenly, the word *reward* flashed in my head. A reward to bring Pearl home! I'd brought Pearl home before, but for free. This time I'd get paid for it. I needed all the money I could get. "Mrs. Dingle is *really* giving a reward to get Pearl back?"

He sniffed and nodded.

I patted him on the back. "Cheer up, Jeffrey Dingle, today is your lucky day!"

9 🐾

Jeffrey got off the elevator and ignored me.

"Hey, wait up." I ran after him. "Do you know I'm going to be a real live detective someday just like Detective Jasper in *The Double Trick Caper*?"

Jeffrey kept walking.

"And that someday I'm going to be the chief of detectives, the most famous crimestopper since . . . Sherlock Holmes!"

He unlocked his apartment door and shut it behind him, right in my face. The nerve! I folded my arms and waited. A few minutes later, he came out with his books on top of the stack of papers.

"I even have a theme song." As we walked to the elevator, I sang, "Be it dog, or cat, or gerbil, chicken, I will find it if it's missing."

While we were going down on the elevator, he didn't

say a word. Something nagged at me again. I couldn't figure out what. I changed my book bag from one hand to the other, then wiped my sweaty palm on my jeans.

"I know you're mad about the time I ruined your lunch. You must've been starving all afternoon."

He rubbed his stomach. "Who starved? I ate it."

"Spaghetti with butterscotch pudding sauce?" I gagged. "Please, Jeffrey. I know I can find Pearl. I *know* it."

Jeffrey broke out into giggles. When he stopped giggling, he said, "Okay, you're hired." He dumped the rest of the signs in a trash can on the corner. That was too easy.

"About the reward," I said. "I think, since I'm . . ."

He cut me off and said, "It's *all* yours."

I pulled his arm. "What are you talking about? How much is this reward? Two cents or something?"

"No. Two hundred dollars."

"Two . . . ! Yeah, sure. And it's all mine? Yeah, uh huh. How come?"

He hunched his shoulders. "I . . . I . . . I just want Pearl back."

"Yeah, sure." I didn't realize Jeffrey had become so attached to Pearl.

"If you don't want to . . ."

"Did you hear me say that I didn't want to? All I'm saying is you better be telling me the truth." I poked my finger right at his face. His eyes crossed. "I swear, Jeffrey Dingle, if you're lying to me, you'll regret it the rest of your life." I adjusted my book bag.

"We'll take down all the other signs," he said. "Then it's just you and me."

I gave him a squinty, narrow-eyed look.

"We make a great team!" he said. He yanked a sign off a streetlight pole. "Greater than great!" Down came another one.

"I'm not part of any kind of team with you." I started walking faster. But his legs were just as long as mine, and he kept up just fine.

"We're going to be the best detective team since Holmes and Watson."

"Not on your life," I said.

"Wait till we solve The Case of the Missing Pearl."

"The Mysterious Disappearance of Pearl," I said.

"I like The Case of . . . and I think we should—"

"I'm the boss. I say it's The Mysterious Disappearance . . . and furthermore, *I'm* going to solve this ca— crime. *I'm* going to collect all of the reward. So why don't you just go away and let me take care of everything?"

"Pearl's my dog," he squeaked. "And if I don't w-w-w-work with you, I'll, I'll l-l-l-leave the signs up, and the whole world will be l-l-l-looking for Pearl."

"The whole world, my foot." But I could not chance someone else finding Pearl and getting that two hundred dollars. So I finally gave in to him. "But remember one thing. I am the boss, the chief. I'll make all the decisions."

"Roger," he said with a salute, then wiggled his ears.

"I wish three o'clock would hurry up and come. Pearl could be sick or hurt."

Or dead. I shuddered. I was anxious to get started. But when it was time to leave school, something terrible happened. Ms. Leslie kept the whole class in. The homework the night before had been to choose a topic for a paper and make an outline. Everybody flunked, including Roxie. Roxie's mother did her outline.

"I can't stay," Helen said.

"I have to go shopping with my mother," Jorge said, like he was giving Ms. Leslie a warning.

"And I have to pick up my little sister," said Vicky, who didn't have a little sister.

"And I got a—" Jeffrey nudged me, and I kept quiet. I wondered why he nudged me. I was probably the only one telling the truth. I did have a dognapping case to solve. I might be on the trail of a vicious and dangerous gang. And Jeffrey spoiled my big chance of telling everyone. Ms. Leslie was starting the lesson.

"Noel," she said. "Give us a topic to outline."

Noel slouched down in his chair and grumbled. "Why I Hate School."

Everyone giggled.

Ms. Leslie sighed. "No one has to stay."

Everyone gathered up their things. Above the noise of books being closed and packed away, Ms. Leslie raised her voice and continued, "You all have a choice. We stay until three thirty and do the work"—she paused for a long time so no one would miss this last part—"or, you can take an F right now."

Notebooks were pulled out of book bags. Everyone sat up and paid attention.

Pleased with herself, Ms. Leslie smiled and said, "Good. We understand each other." She then wrote Noel's topic on the board. Her chalk made those horrible scratchy noises. I winced. I hated sitting there when I could be out doing something important.

"Now, who can give me a good subtopic?" Ms. Leslie asked.

Every hand in the room shot up.

By the time Ms. Leslie let us out, it was almost four o'clock. Not a soul was left in the school except for the janitor, who was cleaning up the rooms.

As we were leaving the building, Noel grumbled, "She's like a warden."

"Eight more months of her," moaned Vicky. "I can't take it."

"Me either," said Roxie. "Let's go to my house."

It was gray and cold out. Thick, dark clouds covered the sky. It looked like winter already. This was going to be the worst winter of all. There would be no skating in the park with my best friend, no throwing snowballs, no fighting and making up. I missed Wei Ping.

Why did it have to be this way? Here I was with Jeffrey, while everyone else had a best friend. At first, we just walked without talking. I stared down at the pavement.

"I didn't tell you about Cleo. She's this beagle. She's black, white, and brown. I love her, and I'm going to buy her."

"She's why you want the reward money?" he asked.

"Uh huh."

"Then we better get started," he said.

I elbowed him. "That's my line. I'm the chief, remember?"

"All right," he said.

"Take me to the scene of the crime."

"Roger!" He saluted me.

Brother!

"I'll pretend this is Pearl." He stuck out his arm like he was walking an invisible dog. People gave us strange looks as we walked down the street. I tried to pretend I wasn't with him, but that was hard. He kept saying, "Wait up, Chief."

We stopped in front of our building.

"Now what?"

"Auntie was out of rolls and instant coffee. I was taking Pearl on her regular evening walk when I remembered the rolls and coffee. I went over to this parking meter." It was the one directly in front of Connie's Bakery. "I tied Pearl's leash around it like this." He tied the imaginary leash.

A woman carrying a bag of groceries walked over to us. "Caught you!" She grabbed my arm. "You're the ones been letting air out of my tires."

I swallowed. "We were only . . ."

"Don't play innocent. POLICE! POLICE!"

Jeffrey gave me one sharp tug. I was free of her. Some of her oranges fell out of the bag and went rolling under her car. We had to get away. But where? "M-M-M-Mr. G's," said Jeffrey.

We ducked into Mr. G's store. Killer barked at us, saliva spraying from his mouth. He kept dashing back and forth until Mr. G quieted him.

"I smell trouble," Mr. G said as he plumped up a dusty chair cushion.

The woman was still outside yelling for the police, who never came. We heard her car door slam, then the scrunch of her tires as she drove away. I imagined big, juicy oranges getting all squashed.

I drew a long breath of relief.

"That was close."

"Sure was," said Jeffrey. We both broke into giggles.

"You into some kind of devilment?" asked Mr. G.

"Have you noticed anything weird going on around here?" I asked him.

He scratched the stiff hairs on his chin. "A man came in about two today."

"A man?" I asked. "What did you notice about him exactly?"

"He bought that three-legged chair. The one I intended to junk."

"I meant a different kind of weird. Like, did you see Pearl today with someone besides Mrs. Dingle or Jeffrey?"

"Don't tell me Pearl's run away again."

"Not run away, Mr. G. Dognapped."

"Did Annabelle call the police?" he asked.

"*I'm* conducting this investigation," I said importantly.

"I figured as much," he said. "If you ask me, the police ought to be notified before it's too late."

"Police?" I asked. "What for?"

"Longer a dog's missing, the harder it is to find."

"But I know I can find Pearl. I just know it. Please, don't tell Daddy or Ma. I got to get that reward by tomorrow."

He scratched his chin, thinking. "I don't like this at all. So promise if things look the least bit dangerous, you'll come here to me."

"I promise, Mr. G. We better go now. Got a lot to do."

"Then I better walk Killer myself," he said.

I had forgotten all about that. No wonder Killer barked at me. I apologized to Mr. G and promised to walk Killer right away. He said he'd do it, but I said no. After all, we had a deal. Fair was fair.

As I walked Killer, Jeffrey and I finished going over the night of Pearl's mysterious disappearance.

"I went into the bakery. I didn't take my eyes off Pearl for one second. Then I asked Miss Connie to keep an eye on her while I went around the corner to the grocery store."

"And she said okay?"

He nodded. "I ran around the corner, got the coffee. But when I came back, Pearl was gone. I went into Miss Connie's and asked if she'd seen anyone take Pearl."

"Of course she said no."

"I remember her words exactly. She said, 'That's funny, Pearl was there a minute ago. Must've gotten loose somehow.' Then she shrugged her shoulders and tended to her customer. I asked everybody on the street. No one saw anything. Not a thing!"

His eyes were shiny, and his shoulders were shaking like jelly. I was scared he was about to cry. I said, "The first rule of being a detective is to stay cool, calm, and collected." I didn't know what *collected* meant, but I heard it on a deodorant commercial once and it sounded good. "And if you can't, I'm taking you off the case."

He pushed up his glasses and gawked at me.

"I mean it. Now pull yourself together. Head up, shoulders back."

He grinned. We leaned on a car while we tried to figure out who would have the nerve to take Pearl from the parking meter. Killer sniffed the papers and bottles in the gutter.

"Suppose it's a total stranger?" Jeffrey asked.

"Impossible," I said. "Eighty-nine and a half percent of all crimes are committed by people who know their victims."

"Wow." His mouth dropped open. "Where did you learn that?"

"Some book," I said. I made it up, but it sounded like it was probably true. "And do you think Pearl would go with a stranger? I mean, without barking her head off?"

He jumped away from the car. "So someone who *knows* Pearl stole her. Someone who knew I was in the store." He looked up at me. "What do you think?"

"Why do you always steal my lines?"

"I think we should go back to the bakery."

I glared at him.

"That was your line too?"

"In one second, I am going to scream." I yanked at Killer's leash and took him home to Mr. G. Then I led the way to the bakery.

10 🐾

Miss Connie was waiting on a man when we came in. Other customers were waiting. "I'm busy, children," she said.

The store smelled of warm, freshly baked bread. My stomach rumbled at the sight of the crusty loaves. I realized how hungry I was and wondered what Daddy was cooking. Something good, I hoped.

When all the customers finally left, Miss Connie stomped down to the end of the counter where we were standing.

"I told you, I'm busy. Now what do you want?" She wiped her hands on her starched white apron.

"A brownie," I said. They were on sale for half price.

"No, we don't," said Jeffrey. Then I stepped on his foot. "Oh, yeah, I forgot." We pretended to fish around in our pockets for some money. All I had was a hard piece of bubble gum and a pocketful of dirt and bits of paper.

"Just what I figured," she said. "You don't want to buy anything, do you?"

"No, ma'am," said Jeffrey. "I want to ask you about Pearl."

"I told you last night. I didn't see a thing." Once again she wiped her hands. Were they sweating? People's hands sweat when they are nervous. Why was Miss Connie nervous? Did she know something about Pearl's disappearance that she wasn't telling? And why was everything in the store on sale today?

I gave her my narrow, squinty-eyed look. I thought she looked even more nervous.

"I got no time for this chatter," she said. "I'm closing early. Got to clean up." She fussed with a half-empty tray of cookies.

As soon as we left the store, Miss Connie made a dash for the telephone. While she talked, she shook her head, then nodded it a lot. When she hung up, she ran her fingers through her gray hair as if she didn't know what to do next.

"That's a guilty person," I said.

"What if she's innocent?"

"She's the dognapper all right. We just got two problems."

"No proof is one," Jeffrey said. "Two, how are we going to make her give Pearl back to us? If she really stole her?"

"Are you finished yet, *Inspector*?" I folded my arms and tapped my foot.

He grinned. His ears wiggled. "Don't tell me those were your lines too."

"No," I lied. "But somehow we got to find out where she's hiding Pearl."

"Roger."

Then and there we put Phase 1 of *my* plan into action. We squatted down behind a parked car and waited. Cars zipped past us. Stray dogs sniffed at us, but we kept a watch on Connie's Bakery until Miss Connie turned the lights out. She locked the door, then walked down the street. We were hot on her trail!

We tagged after Miss Connie for two blocks. The hairs on my neck prickled and my heart beat faster.

When Miss Connie went into the supermarket, we followed her up every aisle. We watched her dump cans and boxes of stuff into her cart. Once, she turned around. We jumped back. I pulled Jeffrey down. "Stay low," I hissed.

"I can't see." He gave his glasses a push, and I grabbed his arm back down. He stumbled into the display of Green Giant green beans. All the cans tumbled to the floor along with our school books. The rings of my looseleaf burst open and papers went everywhere.

"Look what you did," I said, pushing my papers back into my notebook any which way.

"Me?"

"Help me!"

We were almost done with my notebook when I saw a pair of black combat boots approach. They stopped in front of me.

"What are you kids up to?" It was the store manager.

"*Up* to?" I asked, still down on the floor, scared to stand now. "Two boys came tearing through here and pushed us into your cans."

"Wise guys, huh? Pick up every can and stack them the way you found them."

"What if we can't get them back *exactly* the way we found them?" I asked.

His big, hairy nostrils flared. My knees wobbled. But Jeffrey tugged at my sleeve and said, "Let's just get it over with." He glanced up at the manager. "We'll stack them exactly the way we found them."

"Smart kid." The manager walked away.

We stacked the cans as best we could, as fast as we could. Neither one of us blamed the other, but in a way, I knew it was my fault for being so bossy. When we finished, we sneaked to the front of the store. Miss Connie was at the check-out counter thumbing through a magazine. Then she thumbed through another one.

"I can't make up my mind," she said. Her bag of groceries was already packed. The cashier waited to ring up the total. Finally, Miss Connie took both magazines. "I have a long trip ahead of me."

We were easing out the door because the manager was on his way to see how we'd stacked the cans. We saw Miss Connie sidestep out of the check-out aisle, then hurry to the back of the store. We dashed outside the store, but peeked through the glass to see what was happening. Miss Connie returned to the front of the store, carrying something that made Jeffrey's and my eyes bug way out.

She brought to the counter one can of Tasty Nuggets dog food. That is the same kind Pearl eats! I would have known the label in the dark because that's what I planned to feed Cleo.

"Hot dog!" I rubbed my hands together. "The case is solved."

Jeffrey pushed up his glasses. "What if she has her own dog, and Pearl is still lost?"

"Trust me. Miss Connie has Pearl. I'm sure of it."

A few minutes later, Miss Connie came out of the store. Jeffrey pulled me aside just in time, and we ducked behind a pile of boxes. "Now all we do is follow her home."

He nodded. I patted his shoulder. "We're going to get Pearl. Wait and see."

Jeffrey was quiet for a while. Then he said, "Suppose Miss Connie d-d-d-doesn't have Pearl?"

"She does. So quit worrying. That's an order. Look."

Miss Connie had stopped at the bus stop. A rickety old bus rumbled to the curb.

"Oh, no," Jeffrey moaned.

"Come on." I tagged him and raced to the drugstore to look up her telephone number and address in the phone book.

"You know her last name?" Jeffrey asked, breathing on my ear.

"I haven't the . . ." The answer flashed in my head. "But I know where to find it."

We went straight to Jeffrey's house. Mrs. Dingle's whole apartment was a lot like ours except for the way it was furnished. Mrs. Dingle had a lot of old stuff, like the fancy sofa with the curved legs. Mr. G claimed she practically stole it from him because she bargained him down on the price so much. Over her oval-shaped dining room table hung a blue and white chandelier. Her off-white carpeting was dingy and worn out in spots. I thought landladies were rich. I guess I was wrong. In a way, it was kind of sad she'd have to pay so much money to get Pearl back.

The saddest sight of all was Pearl's food and water dishes on the kitchen floor, filled with Pearl's favorite beef and cheese dinner and fresh, clear water ready and waiting.

"She did that last night too," said Jeffrey. "She threw everything out this morning, then put fresh food and water out all over again."

"Gosh." Poor Mrs. Dingle! Too bad her wishing couldn't bring Pearl back home. I got a knotted-up feeling thinking how it would be if Cleo ever left me.

"We got to work fast," I said.

Jeffrey put his finger to his mouth. We listened. Bathroom water was running. Until now, we hadn't known that Mrs. Dingle was home.

Very quietly, we tiptoed into Mrs. Dingle's office. It was furnished with stuff from Mr. G's shop. We put our books on the rolltop desk that stood by the window. On the other side of the room was the old wooden file cabinet. The top drawer was labeled Tenants' Files.

"You sure my aunt wrote Miss Connie a letter?" Jeffrey asked as he opened the drawer.

"Positive. I remember Miss Connie saying, 'I'm going to do it now.' Sounds to me like she intended to do something terrible."

He started to say something but stopped. We were both absolutely quiet. Mrs. Dingle had shut off the bathroom water. She'd be out any minute now.

"There's not much time," I said.

The drawer was crammed with files, and we went through every one of them. I recognized names of all the tenants. Everyone had a file, including Mr. G and us. But where was Miss Connie's file?

"Jeffie?" Mrs. Dingle called from the bathroom. My

knees buckled under me. She couldn't catch us going through her things.

"Quick," he said.

"I can't find it." I pushed back a thick file, then another one. It was useless. I was never going to find it.

"Jeffie!" Mrs. Dingle called again. Jeffrey poked his head out the door and answered her. "Any calls about Pearl?"

"No, Auntie," he called back. When he got back to the file cabinet, he was shaking. "We'll n-n-n-never f-f-f-find it."

There was just one file left. It said Connie Wise. "Bingo," I said, and tugged on it. Miss Connie's folder was thick and bulgy with papers. Just when I feared Mrs. Dingle would come out and catch us going through her papers, I got lucky. I found a letter right in the front of the file.

"S-s-s-she's c-c-c-coming. P-p-p-put . . ."

"Read it first," I said.

The letter was short and to the point. It said:

> 141 E. 3rd St.
> New York, N.Y. 10009

Connie Wise
412 Third Avenue, #26A
New York, N.Y. 10016

Dear Ms. Wise:

   I sincerely regret to inform you that due to increases in fuel, maintenance, and repair costs, as of January 1, your rent will be increased to $800.00 per month for a period of two years, at which time we will negotiate a new lease.

   Again, I regret this measure.

> Yours truly,
> Annabelle Dingle

"Looks more and more like Miss Connie is our dognapper. She had a good enough reason. Don't you think?"

"Looks like it. Put it back before Auntie comes." First, I scribbled Miss Connie's address in the back of my notebook.

Jeffrey stashed the file back in place. We stumbled into the living room, plopped down on the couch, and opened our math books, pretending to do homework.

By the time Mrs. Dingle came into the room, I was asking Jeffrey how to change an improper fraction into a mixed number.

I don't even think Mrs. Dingle noticed me or cared about anything other than Pearl. She started asking Jeffrey again about anyone calling.

"It's taking so long." She ran her fingers through her damp, limp hair. Until now, I never realized how gray her hair was. "Not one call. Not one. I just don't understand."

"S-s-s-some-b-b-b-body will c-c-call s-s-s-soon." Jeffrey twisted his fingers around one another. His ears were twitching. He was going to ruin everything. Any second he might spill the whole thing about taking down the signs and how we were after the dognapper ourselves, and I might never get Cleo. Now that we were so close, I couldn't let anything go wrong.

A curious look crossed Mrs. Dingle's face, like she might be connecting Jeffrey's sudden nervousness with the phone calls she'd been expecting. He was going to burst. I just knew it.

I nudged him. "Don't worry so much," I said, gritting my teeth. "You'll get the hang of fractions pretty soon."

He looked at me with startled, wide eyes. "Trust me," I said.

Just then the telephone rang. Mrs. Dingle rushed to answer it. "Maybe it's about Pearl."

"Look," I whispered into his ear. "We're going to get Pearl back in no time. Tomorrow—Phase Two. We go to Miss Connie's house and make her give Pearl back."

He gave me a what-kind-of-a-dumb-idea-is-that look.

"You have a better idea?" I asked, and folded my arms.

"How are we going to *make* her?"

I patted him on the back. "Glad you asked, Inspector, because that is *your* job."

11 🐾

Today was the day! We had to find Pearl or else I would lose Cleo. And from the moment I woke up, everything was going wrong. For one thing, Daddy had decided we all had to leave the house together and go on a family walk. At exactly that same time, I was supposed to meet Jeffrey down in the lobby to set a trap for Miss Connie.

"Everyone ready?" Ma asked. She was in a hurry as usual.

I stalled by taking small bites of egg. I hoped they'd get sick of waiting for me and leave without me.

"Why don't you all go on?" I said. "I'm really hungry this morning." I grabbed another piece of toast.

Ma glanced at her watch, then looked at Daddy. But he was too busy running in place to pay attention to anybody. Now that he was a full-time writer, he acted weirder every day.

Finally, Daddy said, running and huffing, "Up and at 'em."

I kept on eating. How could I trap Miss Connie with my whole family watching me? I had to get rid of them. I dunked my toast into my milk and sopped it up.

"What are you doing?" Drina frowned.

"What's it look like, jerk?" That would get her mad.

"Jerk! I'm not walking anywhere with that creature," she said. "I'm leaving right now." She headed for the door. One down. Two to go. Daddy jogged to her and caught her by the arm.

"We are taking a walk together," he said.

"Let her go," I said. "I rather walk with an orangutan any day!"

Drina came stomping back to the table. "I'm going to deck her."

"You're not decking anybody, Drina," said Daddy. "And you, Olivia, had better finish your breakfast and fast."

I almost choked on the toast in my mouth. Daddy never called me Olivia, except when he was about to blow his top or worse. I gulped down the rest of my milk and got up.

"Never mind the plate," he said. "I'll do it later. Now, let's get a move on."

I grabbed my books and jacket. We all went trooping out of the house. What was going on here? We never did this before.

"Who's idea was this anyway?" Drina asked as we went down in the elevator.

"Mine," Daddy said, his face looking stern, as if daring anyone to say his idea was dumb, which it was. Why were we doing such a dumb thing? I can see taking a walk on Sunday in the park. But walking one another to bus stops and to school—that was really ridiculous. What was Jeffrey going to think about us when he saw us piling out of the elevator? Brother! And what would they think of Jeffrey waiting for me?

I pressed one of the unmarked buttons on the control panel when no one was looking. But the elevator did not get stuck between floors. It kept right on going until it reached the first floor. The doors opened. There was Jeffrey waiting by the lobby door.

I hoped he would pretend not to know me. We could talk later in school.

"There you are," he said. "I've been waiting forever." His voice was so loud, it boomed in the big open lobby.

"Forever?" asked Drina under her breath. She covered her mouth in a giggle. "This sounds like a love affair."

"Shut up," I hissed. I walked over to Jeffrey. "Listen, I'm stuck with them." I nodded over in their direction. They all had smirky grins on their faces. "Be cool about everything. Get it?"

He pulled his shoulders back. "I'm cool," he said, like a TV gangster.

As we walked past the bakery, I noticed how empty it was. Just a few loaves of bread and some rolls on the shelves. That was strange. Miss Connie was usually open by now, selling doughnuts, rolls and coffee. I started to get a close-up look, but Drina had to go and open her big mouth.

"Don't tell me you're thinking about food after pigging out this morning."

"For your information—" I almost spilled the whole story, but Jeffrey stopped me with a jab in the ribs that almost knocked me over, and made Drina burst out laughing.

74

Ma and Daddy, walking ahead with their arms linked together, only turned around and smiled at us. Boy, did they look weird together. Ma was dressed up in a suit and high heels and carrying her briefcase. But Daddy was wearing his running shoes, jogging suit, and a sweatband around his head.

When Daddy kissed Ma at her bus stop, I could have died of embarrassment. He didn't just peck her on the cheek or something. They kissed a long, long time. The bus driver even yelled, "Getting on the bus this year, lady?" That's the only thing that made them stop. Then Drina got on her bus. Her junior high school was uptown. She went to a special performing arts school. Finally, Daddy, Jeffrey, and I were left.

"Daddy, you're not really going to walk us to school, are you?"

"That was the plan, Cookie."

He called me Cookie. Questions were safe again. "Why?"

"We don't spend much time together. This is nice for a change, this kind of experience."

"Yeah, but if all the kids see you like that"—I looked him up and down—"they'll think you're weird or something."

"What's wrong with . . ." Then his eyes lit up. He nodded his head up and down, smiling from Jeffrey to me. "I see." When he squeezed my hand, I knew what he was talking about, but he was all wrong, dead wrong. Before I could tell him how wrong he was, he jogged away.

"I like your family," Jeffrey said on the way to school.

"They're all right."

"I bet your parents never fight," he said.

"Almost never," I said. My parents were the perfect

couple, but I didn't want to go on about them. I had a feeling Jeffrey was thinking about his parents' divorce. He felt bad enough already. I got the subject around to Miss Connie.

"Did you figure out how we're going to make Miss Connie give us Pearl?" I asked.

"Not yet."

"You got until three o'clock."

By three o'clock, it was a lot colder than it had been in the morning. Although it was sunny, there was a frosty chill in the air that bit right through my jacket.

"Gosh, it's cold." I stuffed my hands in my jacket pockets.

"Yeah, like winter," Jeffrey said.

That gave me a shivery feeling, maybe it was because of not getting to check on Miss Connie this morning. Anyway, I kept my worries to myself, remembering what Mr. G always said about looking for trouble. As it turned out, there was plenty to worry about.

When we got to the bakery, a man on a ladder was scraping the words *Connie's Bakery* off the window.

"Hey, you can't do that," I shouted up at him. "Hey, you hear me?" I jiggled the ladder until he grabbed the sides.

"Get away from here." He waved that scraping thing at us.

"Where's the owner of this store?" I demanded.

"You're looking at him."

"Where's Miss Connie?"

"Gone," he said.

"I don't get it. This morning this was a bakery."

"This afternoon it's a sporting goods store." He went back to scraping without another word to us.

"And we just missed her?" I asked.

A miserable look crossed Jeffrey's face.

I felt like crying.

The bakery was gone for good. Not a loaf of bread, rack of cookies, or basket of rolls was left. All the counters were gone, and planks of knotty-holed wood were lying about. Instead of the sweet smells of cookies and chocolate and fresh baked bread, the place smelled of sawdust.

"Get out of there, you kids," the man snapped at us. "This is private property. Don't want kids hanging around."

Walking around a used-to-be bakery wasn't going to get us anywhere. So we left and headed uptown.

"If she's trying to make a getaway, we've got to catch Miss Connie at home," Jeffrey said.

"She has a surprise coming," I said, and linked my arm in Jeffrey's. When we passed the block where the pet store was, I said, "Can we go inside for a minute just so the pet store man knows I'm coming back with the money?"

"Will you show me Cleo?"

"Sure," I said, and we went inside.

The pet store man was feeding the kittens. I took Jeffrey to Cleo's cage. When she saw me, she scrambled to her feet and barked at me like she was begging me to take her home right then.

"She's prettier than you said," Jeffrey said. He tapped the window of the cage.

The pet store man came over, chewing on his toothpick.

"Good news," I said, smiling up into his face. But he was not smiling. "I'm coming for Cleo."

"I close at six thirty," he said. "Not a minute later."

"You won't really send Cleo back, will you?"

"The ASPCA has some beauties."

"They don't have Cleo, and that's who I want. Cleo."

He shrugged his shoulders. "Suit yourself."

"We'll be back," I promised as we left the store.

Miss Connie's building was tall and had revolving doors.

"I bet there're a hundred apartments in here," I said as we went through the doors.

"More," Jeffrey said.

A doorman wearing a gray uniform stopped us. "Where to, children?"

"Apartment 26A," I said.

On the wall was a list of all the apartments and the names of the people who lived inside. He ran his finger down the list. I figured since we knew Miss Connie lived there, it was no sense waiting for him to tell us that. So we headed toward the elevator. The doorman called us back, but the elevator doors were already shutting behind us.

The elevator sped to the twenty-sixth floor. My ears got stuffed. I did not swallow to unstuff them. I liked how it made sounds seem far away.

"This is it!" I yelled.

"I know," Jeffrey yelled back. I guess he liked stuffed ears too. But mine popped open as we walked down the hall.

26A was at the end of the hall. We rang the bell. Miss Connie did not answer. We rang again and again. Still no answer.

Finally we rang the bell of 26B. A boy came to the door.

"Hi," I said.

"Whatever you're selling we don't want."

"We're not selling anything," said Jeffrey.

"We just want to ask you a question," I said.

"Okay, shoot." The boy slouched in the doorway.

"Do you know where Connie Wise is?" I asked.

The boy looked from Jeffrey to me. "Who wants to know?"

"See, we're detectives and—"

He burst out laughing.

"We are. And we're investigating—"

He rolled his eyes. "All right, why do you really want to know about Miss Wise?"

It was obvious he wasn't going to believe the truth. I had to say something. So I lied. I nudged Jeffrey to back me up and help me if I needed it. But he just stood there as if he didn't understand. That was just my luck to be stuck with a dummy.

"See, every year our school votes a person to be Citizen of the Year. We have a special assembly, give a trophy and a corsage."

"Citizen of the Year? In October?" the boy asked.

I elbowed Jeffrey. He stuttered something that made no sense. Then I said, "Yeah, well, see, Miss Wise was *last* year's winner. This year's winner gets the award *next* year. Next October, that is."

I kept elbowing Jeffrey on the sly while this kid kept nodding his head as if he were saying, I'm not dumb enough to believe that. Then I took over again. I had to convince him.

"And the school sent us to make sure Miss Wise is at the assembly tomorrow morning. It's bright and early. So, you see it's important we talk to her this minute."

He laughed. I was sure he didn't believe my story. As it turned out, that's not why he laughed.

"Too bad your assembly wasn't yesterday," he said. "Miss Wise moved this morning."

12 🐾

"That's a lie!" I said. "We just saw her yesterday. You're wrong. Dead wrong."

The boy shrugged. "Have it your way." He started to close the door.

"Hey, wait. Did she have a dog with her?"

"I don't know."

"Where'd she move to?" I asked.

"Don't know that either."

"Don't you know anything?" I asked.

"Yeah, I know I'm tired of talking to you." He started to close the door again, but I stuck my foot in it.

"Please, it's a matter of life and death."

"A dumb assembly? Yeah, sure."

This kid was such a pain!

I elbowed Jeffrey. He pushed up his glasses and asked, "Who would know where Miss Wise moved to?"

"Ask Tommy, the doorman. Now move your foot before you lose it in my door."

"Thanks," we said, and walked to the elevator. As we were going down, I asked Jeffrey, "How come I did most of the talking?"

"You lie better than me." He pushed on his glasses.

"That's cause I practice more," I said. "All it takes is practice. Lots of it. You want to be a detective, you got to learn how to lie when you have to."

"I never lie," he said, and I believed him.

We got off the elevator and went over to the doorman. Before we even asked him one question about Miss Connie, he was ready to tell us everything we needed to know.

"I called you children back. I guess you didn't hear me."

I cleared my throat, a signal for Jeffrey to keep his mouth shut.

"Miss Wise moved today."

"We know," Jeffrey blurted out. I elbowed him hard. He was supposed to let witnesses do all the talking, spill their guts if they had to. I needed to have a long talk with that kid.

For now, I gave him a look, then said to the doorman, "You were saying . . ."

"She moved to Pennsylvania."

"That's another state!" I said. "Where in Pennsylvania?"

"No forwarding address. She doesn't want anyone to know."

"Did she have a dog with her?" Jeffrey asked.

"Sure did. The cutest little thing you ever saw."

"Was it cream colored?" asked Jeffrey.

Please don't say yes, I prayed silently.

"Now, how did you know that?" he asked. "She just got it a few days ago."

That did it! I pushed through the revolving doors. Jeffrey came after me in a rush.

"He might know someone who knows more," he said, grabbing me. "Let's go back and ask."

"What's the use? We can't go all the way to Pennsylvania." I gulped back the tears.

"We can't g-g-g-give up now," he said.

"You got a better idea?"

"Phase Three."

"We don't have a Phase Three. It's over. Finished. Pearl's gone for good. I don't get the reward, and Cleo goes back to the kennel. I'm back where I started, Jeffrey," I yelled. "Nowhere!"

I took off and ran for blocks, until I was too tired to run any more. I knew Jeffrey was right behind me. Finally I stopped and leaned against a building and cried a long time.

"It's getting late, Olivia," Jeffrey said in a quiet voice.

"Go away and leave me alone," I wiped my nose on my sleeve. He stood there. "Go away!" I yelled. "You deaf?"

"I know we're going to get Pearl back."

"Shut up. Just shut up about it, all right?" My eyes saw all blurry from tears. Buildings and passing cars were ripply. I wiped my eyes to see better, but the tears wouldn't stop. In those few moments, I thought of Wei Ping, the kids at school who either ignored me or teased me—I thought of never again holding Cleo's soft, silky body. The tears kept flowing for all the things that were tangled up together. I hid my face behind my arm. "Please go away."

He did not go. He did not say a word. He took my hand

and started walking down the street. I don't know why, but I went with him. We were going home, and on the way he kept saying how we couldn't give up on Pearl. All the while, he held my hand.

"I'm sure we're going to find her," he said.

I nodded, but I wasn't thinking about Pearl at that moment. I was thinking of how warm his hand was closed around mine. I didn't care if the people we passed on the street or all of West Side Free School saw me holding Jeffrey's hand. We didn't drop hands until we got on the elevator. I hated to let go even then.

When the elevator stopped at our floor, Jeffrey said, "Let's go over all the clues again right this minute. Okay?"

"What's the use?" I asked, and went home.

When I got inside the house, the first thing that hit me was the sound of Ma's voice. It was just five o'clock. She's never home before seven or eight o'clock at least.

Daddy winked at me, then leaned his face down for me to kiss his cheek.

"You got flour all over yourself." I brushed flour off his mustache. He was busy kneading dough at the kitchen counter. Ma was home early. We were all together. That felt good.

"Ma took the afternoon off or something?"

"A luxury I cannot afford," Ma said. She'd come into the kitchen. She was tucking a silk blouse into her skirt. It was a different blouse from the one she'd worn this morning. Usually when she comes home from work, she changes into a long lounging dress. That's when I noticed three places set at the dinner table. Ever since Ma got that promotion, there are never four places set, except for Saturday and Sunday. Ma comes home after dinner. Some nights she's so late, Drina and I are already in bed. I hardly ever see her anymore.

She pulled a grape out of the fruit bowl, popped it into her mouth. "Got to run."

"Why?" I asked.

"A meeting," she said. "I won't be late."

"I'll hold the fort," Daddy said. They kissed, and she was gone.

Daddy put the dough into a bowl and covered it with a damp cloth. "We'll let that rise." He took the lid off the skillet and stirred. He was making a Moroccan chicken dish that had lots of spices, onions, and olives in it. He spooned out some of the sauce, holding his hand under the spoon to catch the drippings.

"Taste."

"Can I ask you a question?"

"Let me see now," he said thoughtfully. "This makes how many for today?"

"I don't know. Oh, Daddy." Despite how I was feeling, he made me giggle.

He giggled too. "Shoot."

I bit my lip, not sure if I should ask or not, but I did. "Does it ever make you angry that Ma's never here, or hardly ever, that she's always working and going to meetings?"

"Why should that make me angry?"

"We don't see her anymore. Not like we used to."

"Mama's job is a very demanding one. She gets paid lots of money, but she's under constant pressure."

"What about *us*?" My voice squeaked. "She's got a job with us, too."

He smiled.

"What I mean is . . ." I said more softly and calmly.

Daddy put his hands on my shoulders. "Mama is a very special person, and she loves us all very much."

"Sometimes I wish she were a little less special."

"Are you kidding? Then I wouldn't be cooking this stupendous meal for my two favorite daughters." He waved the spoon through the air with a flourish. That made me giggle again, even though I wasn't really giggling on the inside. He went on to say, "Now, I need an expert opinion on a matter of crucial importance."

"Mine?"

He nodded solemnly, but he was just joking around. He spooned out some more sauce. "Now, would you please taste."

I tasted it. "More saffron," I said. He let me add the orange stringy spice to the sauce. While I helped Daddy make the salad, I asked him, "Daddy, why is it that some people get everything they want and others get nothing?"

"Who're we referring to?"

"No one in particular. But some people never get what they want, or they can't make things go the way they want them to. Why?"

"It just seems that way, Cookie. True, sometimes you have no control over what happens, but most of the time, only you can make the all-important decisions. And they can change your entire life." He popped a piece of cucumber into his mouth and I did the same.

"Like how?"

"Let me put it to you this way. When I was a college freshman, I was so cocksure of myself I believed I was the twentieth century's answer to Shakespeare. So I dashed off my first English composition and handed it in. Guess what grade I got."

"A+?"

He winked. "You're a doll. No, I got an F."

"You? Fail? You never fail. Nobody in this house does. Except . . ."

"We all fail now and then," he said, soft and comforting. "And we have successes too."

"I know you didn't flunk out. So what happened?"

"For weeks I refused to write a word. I felt miserable."

"Like you wanted to throw up?"

"Worse," he said. "Then one day, my professor called me into his office and told me to either start handing in my assignments or drop out of his class. That would mean I'd be locked out of all the other writing classes. It was then I knew how much I wanted to write."

"Then why didn't you become a full-time writer before now?"

"It takes a whole lot of courage to quit a job that pays money. Writing doesn't pay for a long while. I have a responsibility to you all, and if it weren't for Mama's job and everybody's support, I wouldn't be . . ."

"You mean you've been waiting all this time?"

"It's not that cut-and-dried, but I guess you can say it's something like that. In between the waiting was a lot of living, experiencing." He kissed me on the forehead. "And loving. Now, I think this salad is perfecto!"

After he put the salad into the refrigerator, Daddy went into his study to work some more. I went into the living room to do my homework. I was unable to concentrate because I kept thinking about Cleo going back to the kennel and how I would never cuddle her and play with her. That was one of the things I had no control over. And the talk with Daddy didn't help all that much because I couldn't accept what was going to happen to Cleo. It still seemed like everything went right for everyone except me. For Ma, Daddy, and Drina. But what *I* wanted and cared about slipped right through my fingers. Yet, feeling sad about losing Cleo wasn't doing me any good now. I tried to push her from my mind and begin my social studies homework.

It was past five thirty when I started the last assignment. I needed the dictionary, which was on the bookshelf in my room.

When I went inside, I stopped just at the door, dumbstruck. Drina was kneeling down on the floor, her back to me. But her head was turned sideways. She pressed her face lightly against the pillow she held in her arms. She was pretending the pillow was Tony's dead body. Her cheeks were streaked with tears as she said her final lines in the play. In a shaky voice, she sang, " 'Hold my hand and we're halfway there. Hold my hand, and I'll take you there. . . .' "

I couldn't take my eyes off her. Listening to her say the lines and sing made my chest get all tight and achy just like it did when I saw the movie *West Side Story.*

Drina laid the pillow down gently, stood up, and walked away, her head hanging. When she reached the closet, she realized I had been watching her. She folded her arms like she was getting ready for me to make some mean joke about her acting. For the first time, I realized Drina wasn't as sure of herself as she pretended. She needed people to like her and be proud of her just like everybody else did. She'd never admit it, though. In a haughty-sounding voice she said, "Well, what's your problem?"

"Nothing. It's just . . . you sounded so real."

Her forehead wrinkled as she slowly unfolded her arms. "That *is* a compliment, isn't it?"

"I'll say."

"Thanks, Olivia."

I got the dictionary and closed the door. I went back into the living room and sat down on the couch. Twenty minutes to six. Why did I keep looking at the dumb clock? What good was it doing? I thumbed through the dictionary looking up words and trying to make sentences using them. The house was so quiet. With the door to our room closed, I couldn't hear Drina. Even Daddy had stopped typing. That's why I heard the noise. I got up and tiptoed to the front door. I pressed my ear to the cold metal and listened. There was something out there. Ticking.

13 🐾

Tickticktickticktick. . . . The sound grew louder and louder. I peeked through the peephole. No one was out there. I inched the door open. There it was. On the floor was a small alarm clock. An envelope with my name printed on it was taped to the clock. I pulled the envelope off and tore it open.

> YOU KNOW WHO THE DOGNAPPER IS NOT.
> DO YOU KNOW WHO IT IS?
> ACT FAST.
> FIND PEARL BEFORE IT IS TOO LATE.
> YOUR TIME IS RUNNING OUT ! ! !

It was now twelve minutes to six. The clock was set to go off at six o'clock. What did that mean? What was going to happen in twelve minutes?

I tiptoed to the telephone, careful so neither Drina nor

Daddy would hear me. I dialed Jeffrey's number. I was in luck. He answered the phone. "You got to get over here. Fast. You were right about Pearl. We are going to find her." I hung up, then went out into the hallway, easing the door closed behind me. I waited for Jeffrey for what seemed like a long time.

When he read the note, his eyes practically popped. He gulped so loud, it sounded like he had swallowed a whole orange.

"That t-t-t-ticking," he said, "l-l-like a b-b-bomb."

"What are we going to do now?" I asked.

"D-d-d-don't touch it," he said.

"I already did; I took the note off." I thought about it. "Maybe it's just what it looks like, an old alarm clock." It was made of metal, stood on four short legs, and had a round face. I was almost sure it wasn't a bomb, but the most important clue the dognapper was trying to give me. Number one, Miss Connie was not the dognapper. The note made that clear. Two, whoever the dognapper was, he or she was close by and knew I was searching for Pearl.

The ticking seemed to get louder and faster.

ACT FAST. YOUR TIME IS RUNNING OUT ! ! ! I read it over and over trying to figure out what it really meant.

"We got to do something fast," I said. "Now."

Jeffrey swallowed. "I-I-I th-th-th-think w-w-w-we should t-t-t-tell M-M-M-Mr. G."

"No time."

"We p-p-promised."

That might be the best thing to do after all, I decided. So I carefully picked up the clock.

"Put that d-d-d-down," he ordered. "Before it goes off."

"Too late, Jeffrey." My heart was thumping louder than the ticking. My insides were jiggling around and my knees felt like limp spaghetti. But I couldn't put the clock down. I didn't think it was a bomb or anything, but I handled it very carefully just in case. I had to get it to Mr. G to see what we should do with it.

"We'll go real slow," I said, holding the clock away from me and taking careful steps down the stairs. We did not take the elevator because sometimes it jerked when it stopped at a floor. But going down the stairs took forever.

"Four minutes to go," said Jeffrey. Sweat drizzled down his face. His glasses got all foggy. My arms felt like they were weighed down with lead. I wanted to fly down the stairs with the clock or throw it out a window. I kept saying nothing would happen. But there was still a teensy bit of doubt that made me wish I'd never started this search for Pearl. Why me? Why wasn't the ransom note sent to Mrs. Dingle? On TV the ransom note is sent to the person the kidnapped person or thing belongs to, not to the detective. We weren't even real live detectives.

My hands got clammy, and the smooth metal felt greasy and like it was going to slip from my hands any minute and crash to the ground. What would happen then? I was too afraid to find out.

"My arms feel like they're going to drop off," I said as we walked through the lobby. The lady in 4B was coming home from work and gave us a strange look.

"We're almost there," said Jeffrey. "H-h-h-hold on a f-f-f-few more seconds."

"I'll try." My arms burned at the joints like hot needles were being stuck in them. New hope of finding Pearl kept me going.

We reached the store at last. Mr. G was inside at the counter adding up his receipts, which he did at the end of every working day. Jeffrey held the door open for me.

"Mr. G," Jeffrey said, his voice shaking. "We got real trouble."

Mr. G glanced up. "What's new . . ."

"I don't know what this is, Mr. G, but it's going off any minute!" I said.

"In less than one minute," said Jeffrey.

"Calm down now," said Mr. G. "Just ease it up on the counter."

"Shouldn't we—" I asked. The long hand made a clicking sound as it swept to the number 12. I put my fingers into my ears and squeezed my eyes shut as the alarm went off with a noisy, ear-stinging clang. The clang pounded in my head, and for a minute I was scared to open my eyes, but when I did, Mr. G had the clock in his hand, turning it over.

"Just an old clock," he said. He shut it off. The clanging still banged inside me.

"Look what else we found," said Jeffrey, showing Mr. G the note.

Mr. G scratched his chin and walked from behind the counter. For a long time he didn't say anything. The place was so quiet, I could hear Killer whining on the other side of the door that led to Mr. G's apartment.

"This is gonna take some figuring," Mr. G finally said.

"Who'd play s-s-s-such a t-t-t-terrible trick?" asked Jeffrey.

"Some trick!" I said. "It was stupid and dumb. Anyone who'd do such a thing has got to be . . ."

"Hold on, Libby Lou, what we need to do is work this thing out sensible like."

"Sensible!" I snatched the note from him. "You call this sensible! I was scared to death."

"I'm sorry," said Mr. G. He laid a hand on my shoulder.

"Not your fault," I said. I sighed. "I just don't get it." I read the note again out loud. " 'Find Pearl before it is too late. Your time is running out!!!' How does the dognapper know anything about me?"

"He's going to h-h-h-hurt Pearl." Jeffrey gulped like he was swallowing rocks. "I kn-kn-kn-know it."

"Maybe he'll come after us too," I said. "And kidnap us too? Oh, Mr. G." Then I turned to Jeffrey. "Why'd you get me in the middle of this in the first place?"

"Me?"

"Yes, you."

"Enough is enough," said Mr. G. "I want you two to just listen up."

"We don't have time," I said. "We got to do something before that crazy dognapper—"

"There ain't no dognapper," Mr. G said above my ranting. The place got real quiet. There was just the sound of Killer's whining. "It was me. I took Pearl."

"You?" I asked.

"But why?" Jeffrey asked. "It can't be you."

Mr. G's eyes met mine for a second. Then he looked down and over at Jeffrey. He settled his eyes on a place on the wall and told his story.

"I didn't mean no real harm," Mr. G said. "But when I got the rent increase notice, I was mad at Mrs. Dingle and mad because you were friends with her nephew. Nothing personal, Jeffrey. I was all alone. And nobody gave a hoot I've been in this shop for nearly forty years, but in a few months time, that sporting goods store is going to come right through that wall over there." He pointed to the wall where the rack of antique clothes hung. "He's gonna knock my wall down. I'll be forgotten, Libby Lou. A thing of the past. Nobody wants to be forgotten. That's why I did it."

I felt confused. I couldn't believe Mr. G was the dognapper.

Jeffrey drew in a breath. "Gosh, that's awful."

"Of course it's awful. A man's got rights." Mr. G pounded his fist into his other hand.

I patted his arm, feeling him tremble. "You've always said you were going to retire, to go back home, lie in the sun, you and Killer, and do some fishing."

"I changed my mind." He went back behind the counter and picked up his pencil and started writing numbers.

I leaned across the counter, looked up into his face. "You said you were getting tired."

"You sound like you want me to go," said Mr. G.

"Of course I don't. And the thing you said about being mad about Jeffrey and me being friends, it was you who told me I should be friends with him."

"People don't always mean what they say," Mr. G said, adding up receipts. He kept on writing his list of numbers.

"Besides"—I sniffed—"you can't leave, Mr. G, you're . . . you're my friend, my very best friend." I sniffed again, but the tears rolled down my cheeks anyway.

Mr. G wiped them away with his big, plaid handkerchief. "In about two minutes time, I'll be closing up." He looked over at Jeffrey.

"We g-g-g-get Pearl now?" Jeffrey asked. He sounded nervous and scared all at once. "Is she in the shop somewhere?"

A grin, a small, cunning grin, passed over Mr. G's

face. He scratched his bristly face hairs. "Now, that's something I'm not at liberty to say."

At that moment, I knew exactly why Mr. G took Pearl. It had nothing to do with the rent, retiring, Mrs. Dingle, or Jeffrey. It had to do with me. It was one of his outlandish tricks, like the time he made his brother's frog drunk so he'd win the contest. That was when he was a kid. He wasn't a kid any longer, but his gray eyes gleamed now the way they had when he told that story. He said he could finagle a solution out of any problem. That's what this dognapping scheme was all about.

Jeffrey was scurrying around the shop, going through closets and drawers, calling to Pearl. "Here, Pearl. Here, girl." When Pearl didn't answer any of his calls, he said, "You g-g-got to tell us. P-p-p-please."

Mr. G had no intention of telling us. He really meant for me to *find* Pearl. That way I could tell Mrs. Dingle the truth and get the reward for sure.

I stared at Mr. G, overwhelmed that he would go this far to help me. I tried to find the words to thank him, but couldn't speak. He looked away, knowing I understood. Then he made a fist and stuck his thumb in the air.

"Go on, Libby Lou. Take Pearl home."

Jeffrey threw up his arms in exasperation. Sweat trickled down his face. His glasses were steamy. "But where is she?" He pulled up a chair cushion, then threw it back down.

I giggled. "She's not in the shop, Jeffrey."

"Then where?" His voice squeaked.

"Follow me." I knew just the spot Mr. G would choose.

14 🐾

We sidestepped through the narrow aisles that led to Mr. G's apartment. When I went inside, Jeffrey said, "I thought you said . . ."

"That's right."

Killer scrambled to his feet and padded over to me. I petted him. He barked at me, then charged to the back door, ran to me, then to the door again. That's where I headed. I opened it. Killer ran past Jeffrey and me, dodging broken pieces of furniture, rusty pipes, and old tires. He stopped at Mr. G's toolshed and barked. He was trying to tell me about Pearl.

"Pearl's inside," I told Jeffrey.

"Why doesn't she bark?"

I took a deep breath and said, "Let's see." Even though I was sure what we were going to find, I was scared. What if I was wrong, and this was all a big mistake?

We went over to the shed, peeked inside. Pearl leaped up and started jerking around. A muzzle was around her mouth, and she was tied up. It took a while getting the muzzle off and untying her, but we finally did. I scooped her in my arms and hugged her. Then Jeffrey did the same and held her. Pearl licked him and barked, happy to be free.

We brought Pearl back into the store. Mr. G closed his book. "See you found her. You two make a pretty good team."

I felt like crying again all of a sudden. "Mr. G, I just want to say . . ."

He waggled his hand and sputtered. "No need, Libby Lou. Go upstairs and collect your reward." He walked us to the door. "Jeffrey, you see that she tells the story the way it ought to be told. Tell your aunt the plain, simple truth. Just what I told you."

"I will," Jeffrey said. Then we left.

Mr. G took a deep breath and said, "I'll close up now." He shut the door, flipped the sign over to CLOSED, and then turned out the light. Strange. It was as though I were leaving his store for the last time.

How I wished he wasn't going away. He'd been almost a grandfather to me. But like Daddy said, there are some things you cannot control. Then again, there are some things you can. Choices. I pushed that out of my head. I just wanted to get Pearl to Mrs. Dingle and get my reward.

Pearl was getting squirmy in Jeffrey's arms, although he held her better than he used to. We hurried into the building.

"It won't be long now," Jeffrey said. Pearl barked. "Your own puppy at last."

"Yeah," I said, and chewed on my lip. "Jeffrey, when your aunt finds out it was Mr. G, what do you think will happen?" I tried to push this thought from my head, but it kept on bothering me.

Jeffrey hunched his shoulders.

"Will she go around telling everybody that Mr. G's a dognapper, a criminal?" That word made me shiver as I pictured Mr. G in police lineups and getting finger-printed and going to jail for the rest of his life.

"If you don't tell, you'll lose the reward. You'll never get Cleo. You heard Mr. G. He *wants* you to tell the truth." He pushed up his glasses. "But he's taking an awful chance."

"For me, though. He knows how I'm dying for a puppy. He did it for me."

Mr. G was the best friend I'd ever had. He would never have stolen Pearl if it hadn't been for me. And Mrs. Dingle must never know he had anything to do with Pearl's disappearance. I had no idea what she would do and didn't want to find out either. He needed me now, for a change. It was up to me to save him from Mrs. Dingle. But could I give up Cleo?

I wanted Cleo so badly. I could almost feel her in my arms right that minute. In a little while she would be mine. She was all that mattered. Right? I wasn't sure anymore.

Jeffrey punched the elevator button. But I said, "Let's walk up. Okay?" He gave me a strange look, but he didn't question me. I was glad. I just needed more time to think this whole thing over. What was I going to do about Pearl, Mr. G, Cleo? I drew in a long breath.

"What's the matter?" Jeffrey asked.

"One more floor to go. Almost there."

The closer Pearl got to home, the more she wiggled and barked. Pretty soon Mrs. Dingle would hear her and be at the door. I'd have to tell the whole story. Mr. G might end up in all kinds of trouble.

Just as I heard Mrs. Dingle's door open, I realized I couldn't do this to Mr. G. Not for Cleo. Not for any puppy. Mr. G meant more to me than that.

"Pearl?" Mrs. Dingle called. Her footsteps were right over our heads. She was coming closer.

"Give her here," I told Jeffrey. Without questioning me, he handed Pearl to me. But I let her slip out of my arms. She flew up the stairs, then down the hall to meet Mrs. Dingle. Pearl's barks echoed through the building. Jeffrey started to run after Pearl. I stopped him.

"We got to let her go." I felt all trembly inside. "Your aunt can't know what really happened. She'll think Pearl ran away and came back on her own like the other times." Jeffrey's ears twitched, but he said nothing. "I'm not asking you to lie, not really."

Still, he didn't answer me.

"I'll do anything," I said. "I'll . . . I'll give up the reward, Cleo, everything. If you just . . ."

He was wide-eyed. "You'd do that?"

I swallowed, and before I could answer, I heard Mrs. Dingle.

"Pearl! My Pearlie, you came back! Oh, I can't believe it!"

Jeffrey ran up the stairs. I followed him. Mrs. Dingle was cradling Pearl in her arms, and Pearl was licking her face.

Mrs. Dingle threw her head back, laughing. "Look who's back, Jeffie. This is the happiest . . ." Pearl barked at her. "Yes, my little poochie, Mama's going to feed you right away." She was bustling down the hall when she suddenly stopped and turned around and stared at us. "Did you two have anything to do with getting my Pearl back?"

It was my last chance to tell the truth, but a picture of Mr. G locked up in jail flashed through my mind. I could never do anything to get Mr. G into trouble, but what about Jeffrey? It was up to him now.

Mrs. Dingle walked back toward us, her eyebrows pinched together. "Something's bothering you, Jeffie. Did you see somebody with Pearl?"

Jeffrey looked down at the floor. "N-n-n-no. I-I j-j-j-just came from Olivia's h-h-h-house." He gulped. "I didn't see anything." Perspiration streamed down his cheek.

Pearl barked and began squirming out of Mrs. Dingle's arms. She laughed. "I better get her inside."

When Mrs. Dingle and Pearl were gone, I said to Jeffrey, "I know it was hard, what you just did. And I won't blame you if you never speak to me again." I realized how much that would hurt, because Jeffrey mattered to me now.

We went to the stairway. I tried not to think about Cleo.

There were things I had to tell Jeffrey. Things that needed telling a long time ago. He might not even listen to me now, but I had to try. I sat down on the cold marble steps, turning all the thoughts over in my head, trying to fit them into sentences.

"Hey, sit here?" I pointed to the small space next to me. I was surprised when he sat down, but I was also glad. He still didn't say anything. "Hey, listen," I started, and the rest came out in a burst. "I'm glad you did all you did, Jeffrey. I mean, even when you first came to my class, like when you offered me some gum, and when you helped pick up the social studies book, even the time you tried to give me your butterscotch pudding. Believe it or not, deep down, all those things made me feel good inside."

His voice squeaked. "You always acted mad or something."

I got that funny, fluttery feeling again, like when he told me he had read *The Double Trick Caper* five times. I just now figured out I really had wanted to be friends with him back then. Suddenly I wanted to write Wei Ping and tell her all about Jeffrey. She wasn't the only one with friends. I'd have to wait until after dinner.

Dinner! Daddy would be looking for me any second now.

"I better get home." I jumped up and got a terrific idea. "Hey, tomorrow, want to go with me to get my deposit back?"

"What if . . . what if Cleo's still there?"

"Oh. Well, I know I'll miss her. But it won't last forever. Anyway, I'm not sorry about it. So, you'll come or what?"

He nodded and pushed up his glasses.

"Okay, then, meet me in the lobby at ten o'clock on the dot. We got plans to make." He raised his eyebrows in a question. "About this detective business," I explained. "It's not always this easy, but I kind of like it. You?"

"Do I!"

"So let's take my deposit money and buy a genuine detective kit. Fingerprint powder, magnifying glass, flashlight, the works."

"Hey, neat! I'll get my allowance. We'll pool our money."

Just then Daddy came into the hallway. "You out there, Cookie?"

"Coming."

When Daddy saw Jeffrey and me together on the stairs, he smiled and said, "Time for dinner." He winked at Jeffrey, then went back inside. I knew what he was thinking, but it didn't matter. I grinned at Jeffrey.

"See you tomorrow," he said. "Ten o'clock."

"Roger," I said.

He stood up and saluted me. I saluted him back.